To Joe
I will always,
one of my partners in
for no other reason because
are like-minded. I sure do
miss you as my
neighbor

A DRY DUSTY WIND

A collection of historic short stories by
award-winning author

Jacquelyn Procter Gray

Jacque

ISBN: 1-4033-8467-3 (e-book)
ISBN: 1-4033-8468-1 (Paperback)

This book is printed on acid free paper.

1stBooks – rev. 01/03/03

Table of Contents

Forward

Sometimes, the story *behind* the story is as interesting as the tale itself. Many times, I've started researching one lead, only to find another that is more interesting, and I've taken a journey far different that what I had planned.

In the story, "Corporal John Stewart," I had been given a stack of old letters rescued by my brother, Donnell Procter. They were written to our grandmother by her younger brother during World War II. I put the letters into chronological order and started typing them out, with the purpose of preserving them before the paper deteriorated any further. By the time I was half into them, I felt very close to John Stewart. He was homesick, worried about his parents, and he was doing the best he could do. As the stack of letters I had yet to transcribe got smaller, I began to get sadder, because I knew what the last letter meant.

Some of these stories have won awards, and most have been published in local magazines. The cover photo is of the home built by Reverend Robert Donnell ("Robert Donnell" and "The Silver Spoon") in Athens, Alabama. During the occupation of Athens by Union forces in the Civil War, soldiers were encamped all around the house.

The house was condemned a hundred years after the war, and slated for destruction. Fortunately, it has been lovingly restored and is open for tours.

Although I was interested in stories about World War II, I shied away from them because of my lack of military background. While interviewing Ed Horton about his famous father ("The Price of Justice"), we began to talk about his own experiences in the war, and I knew I needed to at least try to write it. The result, "Let Freedom Ring," led to recommendations from other people who knew of remarkable World War II stories. One woman called to tell me that she had heard I was writing about one man's experience, but I should write her husband's story, because it was more interesting. Both of those stories are included here. Another man recommended someone he knew, but finished his request by saying, "He's a Democrat though, if that's all right with you."

The World War II stories were sometimes the hardest to write. Even though the events happened over 50 years ago, many of the men I interviewed are still very emotional. To do their stories justice, they must be written while the veterans are still alive. Too many details are lost by not having them to answer questions.

My cousin, Sharon Procter Mescher, sent me letters written to our fathers during World War II. "Cowboys, Operas, and Marines" was the result. I believe the story shows what a unique family the Procters were, classically trained musicians, yet poor farmers. The story even spawned a reunion between family members and former Marines who wrote letters to the brothers.

Readers will also notice cross-references from one story to the next about events and people. While researching for other projects I work on, I oftentimes run across an anecdote about my own ancestors, who settled in Alabama and Tennessee 200 years ago. I've included many of those fascinating stories here, and alienated a relative or two along the way by writing about events carefully removed from the family history.

One of the stories that is most near and dear to me is "A Splendid Little War." It starts and ends with my great-grandmother's brother, Jim Donnell, and their brother-in-law, Kibble Harrison. It also ties into my hometown of Las Vegas, New Mexico, where the annual reunion of the Rough Riders took place. As a kid, I would see these elderly gentlemen at the rodeo held in their honor, but every year their numbers dwindled until they were all gone.

I hope the reader will find the people and events in these stories as fascinating as I have. If you have questions or comments, e-mail me at: JacqueGray@aol.com. If you would like more information about *Old Tennessee Valley Magazine and Mercantile Advertiser*, send an e-mail to: JoShafer@bellsouth.net.

The United States of America vs. Kate Lackner

Rumor has it that Kate Lackner came from up north to Decatur, Alabama as the consort of infamous riverboat captain Simp McGhee. Miss Kate ran the local brothel, well-known to men of every class with a jingle of silver in their pockets. Miss Kate ran afoul with the law in the early days of World War II, but it had nothing to do with the services she offered! She threatened to expose a scandal that could have brought down politicians from Washington, D.C. to Decatur, Alabama.

Miss Kate was known to be a stunning beauty in her youth, and her girls were quite glamorous as well. Young boys would make it a point to gather on Saturdays as Miss Kate's entourage of girls made their way through town in the chauffeured black Cadillac to the local beauty parlor for a little sprucing up before the Saturday evening festivities. Kate's place of business was a well-known secret in the community, and along with the local gambling joint, she could always be counted on by area charities for a sizable donation to a worthy cause. Miss Kate's personal date would have to make a hasty exit however, for when she heard the distinctive sound of Simp McGhee's steamboat whistle as he came around the bend, Captain McGhee expected to spend time alone with Miss Kate.

A retired Morgan County judge tells this story of Kate Lackner, who would have expected trouble from the law as par for the course. This event occurred prior to the judge's forty-odd years on the bench, but it is still a favorite story of many people who knew the characters involved.

Shortages of commodities during World War II threatened the American economy with inflation, at a time when we needed to concentrate on our soldiers fighting overseas. In an effort to curb inflation, prices for goods were fixed at pre-war rates, and government agents were charged with enforcing these rules.

For Decatur Madame Kate Lackner, a different kind of war came to her doorstep when someone turned her name into the Office of Price Administration for selling Coca-Colas for ten cents, five cents over the appropriate rate determined by a government official. Before this fight was over, Washington, D.C. would get involved and Kate would have her way.

She opened the door to her home one day to find herself face-to-face with a man in a dark suit. He flashed his badge, introduced himself, and informed her that he was sent from the Huntsville OPA office to investigate the complaint. The diminutive little lady invited him in and they sat facing each other in the parlor. She patted the neat bun in her hair and straightened the lace of her proper, old-fashioned dress, the absolute picture of a sweet little grandmother. Whether or not the agent knew of her status in the community is irrelevant, or of her rumored relationship with steamboat captain Simp McGhee.

"Let me understand what this is all about," she said in her Southern drawl, "You say I must charge five cents to my customers for co-colas because that was the rate in 1939? Why, I assure you that I have always charged ten cents, even in 1939. Co-colas cost ten cents on the train and at the circus, why is it not appropriate to charge 10 cents at my...ahem...establishment?"

The agent explained to Kate that the train and the circus were not in the business of selling these drinks for a living. Miss Kate went on to explain, "My establishment is not in the business of selling drinks either, we furnish liquid refreshments as an accommodation for our guests." The unsympathetic agent cited her anyway and informed her that she would have to appear in Huntsville and show just cause why her business should not be shut down for the five cent discrepancy.

The unintimidated Miss Kate paid a visit to Decatur attorney John Sherrill, who came from a family of Republican mountain folks. Sherrill, a University of Alabama graduate, used to say, "Except for the Lord Our Savior, President Abraham Lincoln was the greatest human that walked upon the face of the earth." It was not a popular notion among most Southerners *or* Democrats! He was nevertheless respected for his native intelligence. John Sherrill also possessed a shrewdness that overpowered those with the highest college credentials in the courtroom time and again. The Morgan County judge referred to earlier, recalls with admiration that Sherrill was about the only person who could actually spell the word "ptyzic", and even more impressive, he could pronounce it too. (When asked what the word meant, the judge paused thoughtfully for a moment and said, "I have no idea.")

Miss Kate went to John Sherrill's office, a dark dungeon with a pot-bellied stove in the center. The naked light bulb hung from the ceiling on a chain and was turned on by

4

pulling a smaller chain attached to the base. The light in the hall was of the same spartan design. Sherrill suffered from the effects of childhood polio and walked with a limp, his left hand drawn up under his chin. He carried his papers tucked into his pocket and sported a hair style that was not a complimentary walking advertisement for his barber.

John Sherrill agreed to take on Miss Kate's case in the United States of America vs. Kate Lackner. Taking advantage of the delicate nature of keeping Miss Kate's clientele names as discrete as possible, he predicted that he could cause a panic that would accomplish his goal with relatively little effort on his part.

In preparation for the event, John armed himself with a fistful of subpoenas and went to Huntsville to file for the appearance of witnesses who would substantiate his case; the only issue being the question of exactly how long Miss Kate had been charging a dime for soft drinks at her establishment.

When subpoenas began arriving at the homes and businesses of rather prominent men whose stature in the community was based on their spotless reputations, Sherrill sat back and watched as the momentum gathered enough energy to make Haley's Comet look like an ember carelessly flicked off the end of a cigarette.

As the movers and shakers in the surrounding communities found themselves called to testify as character witnesses in the United States of America vs. Kate Lackner, telephones in Washington, D.C. began ringing. Alabama Senators and Congressmen whose road to Washington was largely paved by the greenbacks of men who wished to remain anonymous in this particular court case, turned their attention to the lowly government agent trying to enforce five cent Coca-Colas.

The powers-that-be in Washington listened, and called the Huntsville agent's office. The case was dismissed, and like the many people who left the center of civilization to become lost in the great frontier of Texas never to be heard from again, such was the fate of the poor agent. John Sherrill's shrewdness won once again and Miss Kate continued to sell Coca-Colas for 10 cents.

A Ghost Town Called Dawson

J.B. Dawson's neighbors laughed at him for picking up chunks of coal to burn in his stove when everyone else burned wood. But there in the middle of nowhere, the windswept high plains of New Mexico, a boom town would spring up out of brittle gramma grass and be named for the man his neighbors called "loco."

Dawson is no longer on the map, as if removing the name of it could erase the unspeakable tragedy that happened there. The pair of ruts that serve as a road parallel abandoned railroad tracks and dead end at all that remains of Dawson, a cemetery of identical, freshly painted white crosses that have recorded the whole remarkable story.

J.B. Dawson sold a chunk of his ranch to a coal-mining company, maintaining 1,200 acres for himself so that he could have "a little open space around the house." His wife contracted for the rights to sell all milk for a period of 10 years to the new coal-mining town that was to be established on his vast property. Dawson was a boom town that deserved a happy ending.

As the largest coal mining operation in New Mexico, the town of Dawson became prosperous. The Phelps Dodge Corporation bought the operation, and by 1907, the Dawson Opera House opened. Pay was excellent, the climate was healthy, and before long, 3,500 immigrants from all over the world poured into Dawson where they could raise their children in relative prosperity.

The corporation built identical homes, white with green trim, for the miners' families. Boarding houses were constructed for single men and those saving money to bring their families over to America. The school boasted 40 teachers and the hospital employed five doctors. Residents even enjoyed their leisure time putting on the golf course or swimming in the community pool. The high school had a well-known and widely-dreaded football team. These sons of coal-miners tended to be large kids. If a neighboring town's team happened to win a game against Dawson, they knew to get out of town fast to avoid the wrath of the townspeople. Dawson *hated* to lose.

Just when life for the Dawson residents seemed too good to be true, a catastrophe brought a terrible reality to the growing town. On October 20, 1913, after a two-week

8

inspection, the New Mexico Inspector of Mines pronounced Stag Mine No. 2 "free from traces of gas, and in splendid general condition." Just two days later, at a little after 3 p.m., an explosion in Mine No. 2 sent flame out of the tunnel mouth for a distance of one-hundred feet, followed by smoke and debris.

Three-hundred men were instantaneously entombed.

The explosion rumbled two miles away in the tiny town, and housewives grabbed for their children and frantically ran to the mine. Over the next several days, workers painstakingly dug, hoping for survivors. The crowds of frightened and hysterical family members impeded the rescue process. Rescuers eventually found a dazed mine mule several thousand feet into the pit, and for the first time in days, a ripple of relief and hope ran through the crowd. But when the rubble and destruction were cleared, there were only 16 human survivors. They found men frozen in time, one standing with a pick still in his hand as if he were hard at work. Another had both hands over his face to protect himself from the ball of fire that engulfed him.

The people of Dawson grimly buried their dead and demanded explanations for the catastrophe. The Phelps Dodge Corporation generously gave each widow $2,000, plus $200 for each child, and offered to relocate the families who wanted to return to Europe. An investigation into the cause of the explosion determined that an overloaded dynamite charge had been set off while there were men in the pit - a careless and deadly violation of mine rules.

Safety measures were strengthened, and new miners were brought in to replace those men remembered by white crosses in the town cemetery. Life went on as before, but the tragedy remained in the back of their minds.

Nearly ten years later, on February 8, 1923, Dawson suffered another horrible loss. At about 2:30 p.m., a train of 35 cars carrying fine coal and dust toward the entry of Mine No. 1 suddenly jumped the track and crashed into the wooden beams supporting the tunnel roof. The coal cars toppled as the roof beams fell, bringing down a live wire. A spark ignited the coal dust and the blast roared through the mine shaft. The sprinkler system, which should have at least minimized the fire, was frozen in the cold February air. One hundred twenty-two men perished.

The alarm at the mine was sounded again, but the rumble underground told the townspeople exactly what had happened. As they did back in 1913, the distraught families abandoned their chores to run down to the mine shafts and wait. Their constant vigil was filled with praying, crying, and hysteria.

Two men who were caught in the underground firestorm, soaked their sweaters with water from their canteens and covered their faces, praying as they lay on the ground. They heard distant voices crying desperately for help, until eventually those voices became deathly still. They waited nearly 19 hours for help that never came, and finally began their journey through the black, stumbling over the bodies of their friends, neighbors, and brothers in the mine. They were the only survivors.

An investigation of the disaster revealed human error as the cause. Once again the people of Dawson buried their dead and got back to work. The town newspaper chronicled the effects of World War I, the Depression, and even the tough times in World War II when the young men left Dawson to fight, leaving a depleted work force in the mines. Federal authorities even came to Dawson to confiscate personal weapons from the Italian immigrants, even though they had sons fighting for America! But despite the prosperity that comes from hard work, there were outside influences that led to the final demise of Dawson on April 28, 1950.

Coal was becoming expensive and impractical for industry and home use. Natural gas, oil, and hydroelectricity threatened the coal industry. Even the trains switched to diesel. The cost of coal rose as the coal miners' union called for strikes to demand higher pay. It all became too much, and Phelps Dodge closed the town of Dawson, selling and dismantling everything. The homes were sold and moved to neighboring cities, and the town buildings were razed. Even the trophies earned through the years by the feisty Dawson High School Miners were taken on April 22, 1950 to the Colfax County Courthouse in Raton.

Today, all that remains of Dawson is the cemetery. The crosses speak of the sad reality that brothers, fathers, and sons died together in the mine shafts. The names on the crosses bearing the years of 1913 and 1923 are predominantly Mexican, Greek, and Italian. Because these men did not speak English, they often worked with their own countrymen and therefore died with them too. Not all of the graves contain bodies. Some could not be recovered from the mines and will remain entombed forever.

An occasional visitor still pulls off the highway to find the graveyard at the base of the scenic mesa. The wind still blows through the pine trees, the only sound now where 400 men met their violent deaths. The crosses stand out brilliantly against the rugged mesa, thanks to the men who return every year from the Phelps Dodge Corporation, to repaint each and every white iron cross.

Let Freedom Ring

Lt. James "Ed" Horton, Jr. heard the whistle of incoming German 88 mm howitzer shells and hit the ground face first. As one exploded just beyond him, he felt the rush of flying shrapnel pass above him. He was shaken, he was lucky, and he was just another kid from Alabama sent to fight against Hitler's army.

Ed Horton was a young man from Limestone County, Alabama, attending school at the University of Tennessee. As a member of the ROTC, he continued his college classes until he was called in the Spring of 1943 to attend basic training at Camp Croft in Spartanburg, South Carolina. While awaiting an opening in, and an appointment to Officers' Candidate School, he took classes at Auburn and the University of Mississippi. Finally, he was sent to Ft. Benning, Georgia as a member of OCS Class #328. He graduated from the school in June of 1944, and was commissioned as a 2nd Lieutenant.

Ed was assigned to the 71st Infantry Division, a unique group of men who had trained with pack mules in the

Rocky Mountains of Colorado. Known as the "Mountain Division," the unit was destined for Italy, the reason being that military operations in the mountains there were particularly difficult for tanks, trucks, and other wheeled, motor-driven equipment.

Despite all the planning, and after having been called upon to train in muck and misery, as might be expected of the "military commands," the mules were retired to a pasture in Nebraska, and the division was converted to a regular Infantry Division - "dog-faces." Then too, the tired Italians were so near defeat that the only remaining task for Ed and his fresh comrades-in-arms, was to finish the remnants of a once proud army of Germans and a few Italians.

So, the proud, anxious - though green - 71st Infantry Division never made it to Italy. Instead, they were sent to France. In the dark hours of February 6, 1945, they landed in the port city of LeHavre. The once bristling seaport had been all but destroyed in the actions of the D-Day Invasion. Through the eerie fog of the English Channel, water lapped up on wrecks of transport and cargo ships. War debris floated in the water, and the city lay in ruins. Dragon's Teeth, the iron and sometimes concrete pillars placed in the water to break up incoming ships, had been marked with flags so that newly arriving Allied ships and landing craft might safely maneuver around them.

After months of training, the reality of war, with all its horror, was about to become a ghastly reality.

The French countryside was a curiosity to these Americans. Quaint farmhouses covered with moss, and serene church steeples shared the gently rolling landscape with bombed and burned out buildings. As they moved toward the front, the French people spilled into the streets to welcome them, emotional and thankful, hugging, kissing and showering all with appreciation. They eagerly traded eggs and milk to the GIs, in exchange for American cigarettes, candy, and soap.

The sense of celebration was soon replaced with solemn foreboding as they pushed on toward Germany. On March 11, 1945, the 71st engaged in their first combat with the German Army south of Bitche. The Germans were forced back through the Siegfried Line towards Pirmasens. Pirmasens was captured, and the Americans advanced to the Rhine and waited until their engineers could construct pontoon bridges near Mannheim. Despite harassing mortar, and at times intense small arms fire from isolated Germans, the 71st drove across the bridge through the cover of a smoke screen.

The worn out German Army was willing to give ground slowly, yet surely were not ready to give up the fight. There were fierce skirmishes with pockets of Germans along the roads and in the woods. The first man of Lt. Horton's unit to die stepped on a mine in the narrow strip of land between the two armies known as "no man's land." It was a sobering experience for the green GIs.

As night fell, the Americans of that sector would shine spotlights at an angle up into the sky, where the cloud cover would reflect the light back down on the enemies' camp. The artificial moonlight served well to keep the already exhausted Nazis from much-needed rest. Were that not enough to cause them concern, the lights also gave the tired enemy good reason to know that this fresh pursuer knew of their every move.

Lt. Horton escaped death several times, though men on either side of him were killed or grievously wounded. The bullet with his name on it had not found him yet - a fatalistic view that kept him from being paralyzed with fear. More than once his thoughts turned to the fields of cotton at home. Beautiful those now seemed, and in his mind's eye they stretched as far as he could see. Then too, he remembered and longed for the comforting sound of the

Southern Railway trains that pierced the silence of the long nights.

The soldiers were all afraid. Still though, they kept their hearts and minds occupied with the grisly task at hand. On one particular day, as they moved slowly through a dense forest, a German sniper picked off GIs, one by one. A bullet that penetrated his helmet and went through his skull brought a gruesome and violent end to Lt. John Steinmetz. He was laying flat with the others, and his fellow soldiers fought panic as they tried to determine the direction from which the small arms fire had come. The unit scrambled desperately in search of the killer as he continued to fire with deadly accuracy. After what seemed like an eternity, someone spotted him crouching in a tree. He was immediately shot.

As the American Army moved steadily across the French and German fields and hedgerows, they took thousands of prisoners. Some of the German soldiers were bitter, angry, and arrogant. Some were confused and afraid, yet others were quietly resigned to their plight. No matter their attitudes, it seemed that all were relieved finally to have the terrible load of war lifted from them.

White pillowcases, sheets, and tablecloths were nailed over windows and doorways of German houses as a sign of surrender. The civilians peered cautiously from inside their homes. The faces that looked out were of women, children, and old men. Their young men were dead on a battlefield or far away.

The 71st Division was now part of the Third Army under the command of General George Patton. The 66th Infantry Regiment, along with two other regiments, made up the 71st Division. The 66th engaged and won a fire fight with about 100 crack SS soldiers holed up in the 500-year-old castle owned by the number two man in the Nazi regime - Hermann Goering. The prize was a much-needed boost for their morale.

Lt. Horton was taken into a village one day with an Army doctor. They were led to a house where a German woman lay on the floor, covered in blood. She had picked up a hand grenade and lost both of her hands at the wrists, another now nameless, poor and innocent victim of Hitler's terrible mania.

At Sulzbach-Rosenburg, the GIs came upon a scene that would make an unforgettable impression on them. At the railway yard, a train of locked boxcars contained about 650 Russian and Polish prisoners. They had been abandoned days before and left to die. The appalled Americans arrived too late for many of them. Before the war was over, they were to see many more examples of the German army's totally unfeeling and casual attitude toward human life.

On a sunny day near Velden, Germany, the unit was ambushed. Lt. Horton organized a three-man patrol and advanced under heavy rifle, machine-gun, and pistol fire into a group of houses occupied by German snipers. Several were killed on both sides, and seven Germans were captured. The intense firefight lasted about an hour. For his actions on the afternoon of April 20, 1945, Lt. Horton was awarded the bronze star.

As they arrived at the Danube, the fighting became more fierce. That picturesque river that had been a sentimental favorite in song and history was now the setting of another struggle to survive.

American artillery guns subjected Regensburg, an industrial city on the south bank of the Danube, to night and day shelling that left the city in ruins. The 66th marched into a city that was virtually deserted.

The German army was finally near its end, and for the most part its officers knew of and were resigned to the inevitable. The fight was out of most of them. Hitler committed suicide on April 30, 1945. The oppressor that had caused the death of millions, was finally exposed as a madman to his own people.

At Gunskirchen Lager, the 71st encountered another sickening sight in a copse of pine trees. The Americans, battle hardened as they were, felt overwhelmed at the ghastly scene that had opened before them. One of the many Nazi concentration camps was uncovered, this one containing approximately 15,000 prisoners. The German guards had abandoned these pitiable people four days earlier.

Out of the shadows crept creatures that had once been strong and healthy men, women, and children, now hardly recognizable as human beings. They literally were living skeletons, their eyes were sunken, their faces hollowed in. Many were too weak to raise up or speak, yet weak as they were, their eyes revealed deep emotion and gratitude beyond imagination. Many sobbed and cried. The suffering seen, as with the stench of filth and death of that day, was never to be forgotten by any of the men.

The American officers immediately ordered food and water brought up for the emaciated prisoners. But many would die anyway, their liberation came too late to erase months - even years - of starvation and emotional devastation. The men who had fought their way to this unforgettable scene of misery would never again doubt our decision to get involved in Europe's war. It was morally right.

On May 2, Berlin fell to the Russian Army. On May 7, the 71st Division seized the village of Steyr, Austria. On the same day, the Russian Army arrived from Vienna, separated from the Americans only by the Enns River. It was also the day that German Col. Gen. Alfred Jodl signed the terms of unconditional surrender in Reims. Members of captured German regiments surrendered their firearms and other weapons of war at the local military barracks. Rifles were thrown onto a heap that soon became a seven-foot pyramid of steel and wood. Hitler's army was tired and ready to go back to what yet remained of their past existence.

The war was finally over and millions of people were dead. German citizens - those who remained - quietly cleared the streets, buried their dead, and picked up the rubble that had once been their home. The specter of Hitler and his heel-clicking officers was forever in the past.

In the town of Steyr, clear cold water trickled down from the Alps. It sparkled in the sunlight, rippling and rushing to the Rhine. Lt. Horton stared at it with wonder. Who could explain this quiet beauty of nature co-existing with the devastation that it had witnessed?

The 71st became an army of the occupation. German prisoners were sent home. The allies maintained order and prevented looting, as they set up camps in order that the German civilians be supplied with some measure of food and care.

Civilians forced into slave labor were now free to go. Ironically, they had to be forced onto boxcars for the journey to their home countries. Although they labored against their will, their efforts had assisted the Nazi cause. Little wonder they assumed that they would not be welcomed back home, or worse, shot to death by unsympathetic Russians as they stepped off the trains.

The Russian and American armies were now camped across the river from each other for the occupation. The once dominant feelings that they were allies ended, and the men in arms had come to watch each other carefully and warily.

Everything about the Russian Army suggested extreme poverty. They were from the peasant class, rough-looking, and their clothing was crude. As they became more comfortable with each other's presence, the American GIs would meet the Russians halfway across an old wooden bridge to swap American cigarettes for Russian vodka. In the middle of this bridge, which had been built in the previous century for horse-pulled wagons, was a gate that neither side was allowed to cross.

Ed Horton's brother Don was in a Paris hospital recovering from wounds to his hand, stomach, and leg. Ed went to Paris to see him, as Don by then was well enough to join Ed and their uncle, Brigadier General Edward Chambers Betts for a visit. Betts, a resident of Huntsville, Alabama, was the Judge Advocate General and close friend of General Eisenhower. The three men enjoyed the sights of Paris before Don was sent back to the United States to continue his recovery in an American hospital.

As Judge Advocate General, General Betts played a key role in organizing the Nuremburg Trials held in Frankfurt. Because of his family connection, Lt. Horton was allowed to spend a day at the trial, sitting just a few feet from notorious Nazi war criminals Goering, Rudolph Hess, and von Ribbentrop. Lt. Horton realized the historic significance as he witnessed it.

Tragically, General Betts died unexpectedly on May 6, 1946 at the age of 56. Lt. Horton made it to his bedside in Frankfurt just as he succumbed. General Edward Chambers Betts was the last American soldier buried in the military cemetery at Luxembourg.

Right after the end of the war, Lt. Horton had the opportunity to see one of the most famous and able commanders in the history of the Western World and perhaps the best known officer of World War II. It was with great admiration that he had been posted immediately behind General Patton as he stood on a reviewing stand. Patton was a tall man, but Lt. Horton was not prepared for what he saw that day. Old Blood and Guts was wearing pink fingernail polish!

Members of the 71st Infantry Division had seen combat and the agonies of war at Germersheim, Coburg, Bayreuth, Velden, Sulzbach, Amberg, and many smaller and less well-known towns. They had pushed farther east into enemy territory than any other unit of the American Ground Forces. They helped capture 107,406 German prisoners and liberated thousands held in concentration camps. American GIs asked time and again why the German people hadn't tried harder to resist Adolph Hitler.

Ed Horton was promoted to Captain in January of 1946 and returned to the United States late that same year. He married, and went to the University of Tennessee to finish his degree in animal husbandry. He went back to the farm in Greenbrier where his father, Judge J.E. Horton of the famous Scottsboro Trials, raised Angus cattle. Ed Horton was elected to the state senate in 1963, and served one term. Like most conscientious men, he found that while he was in the Senate, he was greatly concerned about issues at home, and when he was at home, he worried about issues being considered back at the Senate.

Over the years, he lost his wife and one daughter, and is now married to Mary Alice. His two surviving daughters live in Birmingham. He maintains great pride in the cattle he and his son-in-law raise, those being of the oldest registered herd in Alabama. In addition, the two men farm 1700 acres of cotton.

Over fifty-five sultry summers have passed since Ed Horton wore the uniform of the United States Army and saw combat across France and into Germany. Although some memories are now lost in the soft black of the past, he still winces when the horrors of Gunskirchen Lager come to mind. Today, Ed looks out over the peaceful pasture behind his Greenbrier, Alabama home. Black Angus cows, oblivious to everything but the lush blanket of green grass beneath them, wander in the morning haze. The comfort of the cricket's chirp seems to promise another tomorrow.

The world is a better place for soldiers such as Ed Horton.

A Splendid Little War

Jim Donnell studied the face of the impatient conductor as the train engine idled. "Well Jim, are you coming with me to Cuba, or not?" his brother-in-law Kibble Harrison called again over the noise of the train. Jim was standing outside his sister's Greenbrier, Alabama home holding a load of firewood for her cookstove. He shifted his weight as he pondered his choice. He could stay here in his life of boring predictability, or he could go to a foreign country and experience exciting adventures at the expense of Uncle Sam. The train slowly rumbled forward.

"Ah, to hell with it!" he said as he threw his load of wood on the ground. Without stopping to tell his sister good-bye, he started running for the train.

When Teddy Roosevelt brought his Rough Riders through the Deep South on their way to Tampa, they were greeted by cheering crowds eager to shower them with support and admiration. Ladies brought pails of milk and fresh fruit, and smiling young girls asked for buttons and cartridges as souvenirs from the soldiers. Tired old men who had fought for the Confederacy cheered the flag of the United States, because more than three decades after the Civil War, they were finally proud to be Americans. Only the old women did not smile at the joyous celebration around them. Looking into the exuberant faces of men eager for the smell of gunpowder, they saw the reflection of husbands, brothers, and fathers who never came home from the Civil War.

In early 1898, escalating hostilities between the Cubans and Spaniards threatened to turn into a full-scale war. The United States sent the battleship *Maine* down to Cuba. An explosion aboard the *Maine* sunk it on February 15, 1898, killing 260 aboard.

America's involvement in the Spanish-American War was blamed on William Randolph Hearst, who used the crisis as a vehicle to showcase yellow journalism at its worst. The cause of the sinking of the *Maine* was never determined, but Hearst smelled a story that would sell, and with the encouragement of sensational newspaper reporting, Americans demanded nothing less than revenge. On April 25, the United States declared war on Spain.

Teddy Roosevelt was Assistant Secretary of the Navy at this time. He and good friend Leonard Wood were promoting U.S. involvement in the crisis, and in order to personally participate, Roosevelt resigned his position to raise a company of rugged fighters from the frontier of the wild and woolly West. Wood became the Colonel of the First Volunteer Cavalry Regiment because he had military experience that Roosevelt lacked; Roosevelt took the second-place command as Lieutenant Colonel. Worried that they would not have enough volunteers to fill a regiment, they were surprised when they were inundated with applicants, many of whom were turned away. What they ended up with was a curious mixture of lawmen, ranch hands, ex-cons using aliases, and even more unusual, Roosevelt's former Harvard classmates who spent their leisure time atop polo ponies. Applicants from Princeton and Yale, along with members of the elite Knickerbocker and Somerset men's clubs rounded out the group of Easterners destined for the training camp in the untamed Southwest. These Ivy League dandies converged in San Antonio for training with tough and rugged cowboys who had nothing in common with them, except how to ride and shoot, and a desire to fight.

Becoming a Rough Rider was the fulfillment of Roosevelt's fantasy of being a cowboy. Although at first they resisted the name, newspapers and even military communiqués referred to the First Volunteer Cavalry

Regiment as the Rough Riders, and the name was finally adopted by them as well. After extensive training in San Antonio, the unit developed a cohesiveness that would keep them together well into the next century.

After months of training on horseback, their efforts were for naught. The horses had to be left behind at Tampa because of inadequate transport facilities.

Americans were once again headed for war and this time, North and South alike had a common enemy. Newspapers enthusiastically reported each and every development. The Huntsville Weekly Democrat reported a new item of the American soldiers' uniform. A small flat medal made of aluminum was stamped with the soldier's name, rank, and specifics of his regiment, to be worn around his neck on a chain. For identification purposes in case of death, they are better known by the slang term, "dog tags."

Confederate hero General Joseph Wheeler was a resident of Alabama at the time of the Spanish-American War. At the age of 62, he intended to fight in Cuba. Although by law, he could not hold a commission in the U.S. Army after fighting for the Confederacy, he insisted that he would not be left out. He was actually hand-picked to become a Major General commanding the cavalry Division of Shafter's Santiago expedition.

In a scene that caused his men to do a double-take, Wheeler directed his attack yelling, "We've got the Yankees on the run!" Whether he was suffering from battle fatigue, the yellow fever he had contracted, or the 80-proof whiskey that was used to cure the fever, will never be known.

Huntsville resident Kibble "Todd" Harrison was anxious to fight in the war. He was in the process of organizing a regiment of volunteers from Limestone, Madison, and Jackson counties when he came upon his brother-in-law, Jim Donnell, outside his sister's home in Greenbrier. Jim was a bachelor in his late 30s, and on this particular day, he was out gathering wood for his sister's cook stove. Harrison was on the train that ran directly in front of the house when he hailed to Jim carrying his armload of wood. They did not know it at the time, but they would play a significant role in the destiny of another native of Alabama whose heroism would bring him fame and the Congressional Medal of Honor.

At dawn on June 3, 1898, the Spanish fleet was inside Santiago Harbor off the coast of Cuba. Richmond Hobson, an ensign from Greensboro, Alabama and son of a Confederate veteran, proposed a scheme to sink the

American collier vessel *Merrimac*, which was carrying 2,000 tons of coal at the time. They planned to sink it at the entrance of the harbor, thus preventing the escape of the Spanish fleet and forcing the Spaniards into combat. Expecting certain death in the operation, Hobson and seven other volunteers created an explosion on the ship, while under heavy gunfire from the Spaniards. As the burning *Merrimac* sunk to the bottom of the harbor, Hobson and his volunteers scrambled into a raft, and while still under fire, they miraculously made their way to shore to the waiting Spaniards, including Admiral Cervera, who promptly took them as prisoners of war.

Hobson, who was soon after promoted to Lieutenant, was held as a prisoner in the medieval Morro Castle along with the seven other brave men who blew up the *Merrimac*. Unfortunately, the ship sank long-ways instead of side-ways, and far enough past the channel that the operation was not successful. This detail however, did not dampen America's enthusiasm for the brave men. The New York Times voted Hobson one of the most popular heroes of the war.

On July 6, Huntsville's Captain Kibble Harrison of the 5th U.S. Volunteer Infantry, and Jim Donnell, his 1st Sergeant, were among the men who liberated Hobson and his collaborators. Jim Donnell even acquired a souvenir from the rescue operation, an enormous skeleton key to the door of the Morro Castle.

Another group of fighting men who made their way into the history books was an elite all-black unit nicknamed the Buffalo Soldiers. They were given the name by the Indians because the texture of their hair reminded them of the wild beasts that roamed the Southwest, and also because of the respect they had for the buffaloes and black soldiers. The two infantry and two cavalry units had been assigned out west to keep the peace in areas populated by Indians.

The Buffalo Soldiers cheered when they heard the news that they were headed for the conflict in Cuba. John "Black Jack" Pershing was commander of the all-black Tenth Cavalry. Four men in this unit went on to earn the Congressional Medal of Honor for acts for heroism. They were called "Smoked Yankees" by the Spaniards, and went on to serve as part of the occupation forces in Cuba after the war.

Almost as quickly as it began, in August 1898, the Spanish-American War was over. Cuba was liberated from Spain and the American soldiers, many of whom suffered from yellow fever, began the journey back home.

Jim Donnell came home to Greenbrier with more than just a souvenir key to the Morro Castle. He brought with him something that captured the curiosity of people from miles around - a Cuban boy. The boy, about 10 years old, was visited by folks from all over the area who were eager to see this orphan of war. His dark skin was the subject of much speculation. He wasn't black and he wasn't Indian, so much discussion and examination were required as they pondered the answer. He even took turns living with different families in the area for months at a time. Whether or not he was actually an orphan became irrelevant in light of the excitement of having this young foreigner in their country.

Huntsville, Alabama was quick to extend a helping hand in appreciation of the brave men who fought in the Spanish American War. Poor rations and fever had taken a severe toll on the soldiers' health. Several encampments were established in Huntsville, largely on the reputation of the healthy climate which was reputedly second in the nation only to West Point, New York. Social activities were quickly arranged for the entertainment of America's finest. Moonlight suppers, barbecues, and dances were orchestrated to keep up the spirits of the soldiers.

The soldiers who garnered the most press in the following months were the Buffalo Soldiers of the 10th Cavalry. Although they were segregated from the white troops and had to surrender their arms upon arriving back in Florida, they presented the most impressive figures in uniforms. They were outstanding in local as well as national parades, and attracted many visitors. Although they were not able to escape the obvious racism of the time, they did receive more public accolades for their roles in the war, and their merits were reported far and wide.

By March 8, 1899, the last of the Spanish-American veterans encamped in Huntsville were gone. The souvenir skeleton key which was brought home by Jim Donnell from the Morro Castle, hung on a nail in his nephew's house for over eight decades. The Cuban boy stayed in the area for about another ten years until he left for Birmingham and was never heard from again. The only reminder of the many soldiers who occupied Huntsville, Alabama is a knoll known as Cavalry Hill near the intersection of Pulaski Pike and University Drive. This was the Buffalo Soldiers' camp first named for Joseph Wheeler, then changed at Wheeler's insistence to honor Albert Forse, the first U.S. Cavalryman killed in the charge at Fort San Juan on July 1, 1898.

Lt. Richmond Hobson received the Congressional Medal of Honor and stepped into a future of Alabama politics. Joseph Wheeler entered politics as well, and "Black Jack" Pershing went on to command the army that pursued Pancho Villa and his bandits into Mexico in 1916. Pershing then become a major figure as he commanded the American Expeditionary Forces in Europe during World War I. Teddy Roosevelt's status as a Rough Rider helped propel him into the U.S. presidency as the rest of the Rough Riders went back home to their ranches and bank jobs.

The Rough Riders held reunions every year beginning in 1899 in Las Vegas, New Mexico, because the largest contingent of volunteers came from the New Mexico Territory. Although they met in various cities throughout the Southwest for the next few years, they eventually went back to Las Vegas where they held their annual reunions in conjunction with the honorary Rough Riders Rodeo. The last surviving Rough Rider traveled to the 1968 rodeo from his home in New York, bringing an end to an era steeped in American pride.

The people of the United States gradually went back to business-as-usual, temporarily interrupted by the "splendid little war" and its aftermath.

The biggest accomplishment of America in 1898, was the unity of men from different cultures, economic backgrounds, races, and the beginning of the healing of one nation which, until then, had barely co-existed under the same flag.

Jim Donnell's return to Greenbrier after the war was just as dramatic as his sudden leave on the train. He paused outside his sister's house long enough to gather an armload of firewood. After an absence of more than a year, he walked inside the house, dropped his load of wood and announced to his awestruck sister, "Here's your firewood, Octavia."

As Donnell was dying of throat cancer, he asked two black men to personally dig his grave and pack the dirt over him, when the time came. After his death in 1930 however, someone else was hired to dig his grave at the family cemetery in Greenbrier. After the mourners had left the cemetery, the two black men removed their shoes and commenced to packing the dirt tightly so "Jim Donnell don't come back to haint us."

Kibble "Todd" Harrison died a few years later. It is believed that he suffered for the rest of his life from his bout of yellow fever contracted in Cuba during the war. Both men remained patriotic Americans to the end.

Escape from Johnson's Island

By 1864, the bloody slaughter of the American Civil War had worn on for an excruciating three years. Daniel Robinson Hundley was living in Chicago when the war broke out, but followed his native Alabama into secession. Soon, he commanded the 31st Alabama Infantry. In 1863, he was shot through the hip. He appeared to be mortally wounded, and was left on the field to die. He never fully recovered from his wound, and this fact played an important part in the remainder of this story.

In April, 1864 Hundley heard that his brother William, who also fought for the Confederacy, had been killed. In his diary, he wrote, "In the midst of life, we are in death. Poor brother William is no more. Oh for tears, hot scalding tears to relieve my overburdened heart of its great grief, but I cannot weep. Would that I could lay my aching head upon some gentle trusting bosom and weep myself to sleep as I used to do in my mother's arms when a boy."

Two months later, at the battle of New Hope Church near Kennesaw Mountain, Georgia, Colonel Daniel Hundley led the 31st Alabama into battle with the hair-raising Rebel yell. Facing the enemies' deadly Spencer rifles, they were captured and sent on their way to prison camps. As an officer in the Confederate Army, Hundley was put on a train headed north to Johnson's Island, near Sandusky, Ohio. He felt angry and helpless when he recorded these words to his fellow Confederates, "Courage, then, my Southern brothers! For on your resolute arms and hearts of steel hangs the destiny of millions yet unborn."

The prisoners arrived at Johnson's Island on June 23, 1864. On July 4, he wrote "...there has been no genuine enthusiasm, no spontaneous outburst of patriotic rejoicing, as there used to be in the old days of peace and Union." Hundley wrote in his diary of his despondence at not receiving any letters or news from home and of being "...deprived of the gentle companionship and loving smiles of woman, and of the sweet prattle and innocent mirth of little children..."

In late July, new prisoners brought him the sad news that his old commander, Joseph Johnston, had been replaced by John Bell Hood on July 17. Johnston was so loved by his men that the prisoners wept at the news of his dismissal.

As supplies became scarce, rations for the prisoners at Johnson's Island were reduced to 1/4, or 28 ounces of food per day. They suffered from convulsions and bit their tongues. Around this time, a small dog named Nellie had been welcomed into the prison camp. Nellie became a great help in scaring up the large rats that inhabited the island. The ravenous prisoners ate the rats as if they were a delicacy.

One night, there was a tremendous thunderstorm which Hundley described as a "grand hour of dread sublimity...the booming of cannon" to keep prisoners from escaping through the collapsed west wall of the prison, "and the still louder booming of heaven's artillery."

On September 3, they learned with much heartache of the fall of Atlanta. Rumors of the capture of Early and Breckinridge, and the defeat at Fisher's Hill must have been planted, Hundley felt, to demoralize the prisoners. He responded to the rumor of the death of Union General "Beast" Butler as "...altogether improbable, unless he was assassinated, for he is too base a villain ever to die an honorable death." Hundley frequently wrote of his hatred of Abraham Lincoln and heaped blame on him for every atrocity of the war.

On Wednesday, October 19, Hundley's brother Oscar arrived as a prisoner, after his capture during a raid with Joe Wheeler. Hundley was extremely upset to hear his brother's account of the "blue-coated villains" who had been to their father John's home in Mooresville, Alabama, where they threatened to shoot him while they searched his house for gold. His mother Malinda bravely stood in front of her husband and announced, "Then kill me, too; for the ball that kills my husband must first pass through my body."

In late November, he wrote almost daily of Sherman's barbaric March to the Sea. Grant had ordered that the land be so decimated that a crow flying over Georgia would have to carry its own food to survive. On December 6, 117 officers arrived at Johnson's Island, recently captured at the Battle of Franklin. They carried the sad news of the loss of 1,000 Confederates (the number was actually 6,000, with 13 generals killed, wounded, or captured).

In mid-December, during a full and bright moon, four soldiers attempted an escape over the frozen lake. They were shot.

The presence of constant and painful hunger was more than Daniel Hundley could bear. On January 2, 1865, he got up early and carefully dressed in a Union uniform - composed of various pieces of uniforms worn into the camp by Confederate prisoners. To downplay his 6'3" frame, he wore shoes without heels, and shuffled, stoop-shouldered. He boldly mingled with the Union roll-callers during a fierce snowstorm. As he walked toward the entry of the prison, several prisoners who had been stationed at appropriate posts, began a pre-arranged fist fight. As the roll-callers turned to witness the excitement, only one person continued past the sentinel at the entrance. The young Union sentinel reached over and pulled Hundley's cape from his face, and for a fleeting moment, looked directly into his eyes. Hundley recalled vividly each detail of the guard's face, his bright but dark eyes permanently etched in his mind. As Hundley left the gate and the commotion of the fight behind, he never glanced back. He made his way to the bay which was iced over, and walked in the direction of Sandusky, Ohio, about three miles away. He occasionally slipped on the ice and fell, and as the prison yard stretched farther behind him, he turned for one last look behind him. He felt an instant revulsion of the overwhelming horror he had lived through during his imprisonment.

Daniel Hundley had escaped from Johnson's Island.

Hundley walked into Sandusky, bought apples, and ravenously ate them. He started in the direction of Canada, and the irony occurred to him that this destination was also a refuge for escaped slaves. He wrote in his diary, "Lord God Omnipotent, if it is this to be free, strike when thou wilt the shackles from the slaves of the South!"

Hundley soon discovered that the hip wound he received in 1863 prevented him from covering more than a few miles each night. After walking most of the first night, he located a barn, and because he was familiar with the layout of Northern barns, he made his way in the dark to the loft and dug out a niche to conceal himself. He slept during the day, waking warily when he heard the farmer enter the barn to feed his livestock. He again set out at night across the fields, relying on the stars to guide him. When he ran out of the food he bought in town, he ate shrunken corncobs that remained in the fields after the harvest.

On the third night, he was dismayed to discover that he had not yet found a barn to sleep in as daylight was dawning. He found several barns, but they were all protected by dogs that barked at the limping and haggard stranger, and sent him running in fear. He ran until he was out of the neighborhood and sat down and wept pitifully. Looking upward, he saw a dazzling display of shimmering lights. What he thought was dawn was actually the magnificent Aurora Borealis. Hundley was relieved that he had more time. He finally found a safe barn to sleep in, but after four days of bitter cold, he was physically exhausted and sick. He hopped a freight train and made his way into a city where he checked into a hotel. Because of his physical exhaustion and lingering hip wound, he was unable to walk or stand steadily. He pretended to the innkeeper that he was drunk. After making his way to this room, Daniel Hundley finally slept between sheets, on a real bed, for the first time in years.

The day after Hundley's escape, a $100 reward was posted for him. He was described as 6'2" with dark hair and hazel eyes. A detail was dispatched to the inn where Hundley was sleeping, looking for a different escapee who happened to match his description. The innkeeper directed the provost marshal and clerk to Hundley's room where they examined the official-looking, but forged orders. They were satisfied with the authenticity, but questioned his being AWOL from his new post in Detroit. Hundley sheepishly said that he had been on a "bender" the night before and said that since he had missed his train, he decided to sleep his drunken stupor off and report to his duty at Detroit late, but sober. Satisfied with the explanation that boys will be boys, they next questioned the fact that the buttons on his Union uniform, which had been worn into the prison by his brother after his capture, were buttons belonging to officers, not staff. Again, he satisfactorily explained that the boys were known to put on a little style now and then when given an opportunity. The two men then proceeded to check the remainder of his belongings, at which point, Hundley's hopes sank. They discovered his faded yellow Confederate I.D. He surrendered. As news of the captured Confederate Colonel made it through town, curious people gathered to see him and some town officials came in to talk to him.

When asked by a gentleman about his views of the South and the war, Hundley answered that the "South never could be conquered, that the blood of her Revolutionary sires still flowed in the veins of their descendants..."

The gentleman listened politely, and replied, "But you forget, Colonel, that the American people all come from the same Revolutionary stock and that we of the North are just as brave and determined. The question then narrows itself down to one of numbers and resources."

Hundley then replied, "It is possible that by mere force of numbers, you may yet succeed in conquering the South; but if you do, let me assure you, you will find there only a land of graves, of old men and women and children...but the men of the South will no longer be there to grace your triumph." Hundley was returned to Johnson's Island and his diary was confiscated.

The Civil War ended in April, 1865. Hundley remained at Johnson's Island until his release with the rest of the prisoners on July 25, 1865. Nine years later, he received a letter from a former Union soldier offering to sell his diary back to him. He angrily wrote back that he was "too poor to purchase what was mine by right without purchase." In a few weeks, his diary was mailed to him.

Hundley wrote as his final words in his diary just before it was published in 1874, an unusual apology for the unkind words he wrote about Abraham Lincoln. "Believing as I do in the atoning efficacy of blood, from the moment the assassin's bullet laid low the head of that honored American chief, the writer of these pages has effaced from his bosom every trace of resentment against Abraham Lincoln."

Jacquelyn Procter Gray

Pat Garrett - Lawman from Alabama

Pat Garrett's assurance that he would hold a place in history began one hot July night in 1881 when he fired his Colt revolver. A flash of light and then another! Beneath the smoke and gunpowder, Billy the Kid lay dying on the floor. Little is known of the 6'4" lawman who would later be murdered with a bullet through the back of his skull. But Pat Garrett, buffalo hunter, sheriff, and rancher, was born in Alabama.

Patrick Floyd Jarvis Garrett was born June 5, 1850 on Buckelew Mountain, near the Chambers County, Alabama community of Lafayette. The town was named for the French general who visited the area in 1825.

Pat was named for his maternal grandfather, Patrick Floyd Jarvis, who left for him in his will, his saddle, bridle, and rifle. Garrett's paternal grandparents, John and Jane Greer Garrett, moved to Chambers County, Alabama, located southeast of Birmingham, before 1840.

Sometime prior to 1860 when Alabama census records no longer list them, the Garrett family moved to an old plantation in Louisiana. It was here that Pat's parents died, Elizabeth Ann Garrett in 1867 on her 38th birthday, and John Lumpkin Garrett the next year at the age of 45. Now orphaned at 18, the lure of the Wild West must have been too strong for the Southern farm boy to turn his back. Pat Garrett moved to Texas and became a buffalo hunter. By 1880, he was the new sheriff of Lincoln County, New Mexico. Instead of buffaloes, his prey was the notorious young killer known far and wide as Billy the Kid.

Henry Bonney was a young boy living in New York when his father died. His mother, an Irish immigrant, took her two young sons to Indiana. She met William Antrim, a Union veteran of the Civil War. They married in Santa Fe in 1873 and moved to Silver City, New Mexico. Antrim was a prospector and was frequently away for long periods of time. Young Henry changed his name to William, and thereafter was known by several surnames, McCarty, Bonney, or Antrim. Billy was 14 when his mother died of tuberculosis.

After his mother's death, William "Billy" Bonney made his way to Arizona where he worked in a timber camp. In 1877, he killed his first man for uttering a slur against Billy's mother. He was locked in the guardhouse, but escaped a few days later. Billy was on the run for the rest of his short life.

Billy made his way back to New Mexico and took a job working for a 24-year-old John Tunstall, an Englishman living in Lincoln County. Tunstall was a likable young man, and he made a good impression on Billy. He took an interest in Billy's welfare, possibly the first person in his life to do so. But Tunstall made the fatal mistake of opening a general store in Lincoln, the only competition for another store owned by two Irishmen, J. J. Dolan and John Riley.

Support in the area quickly divided between the two stores. Some were happy to see Dolan and Riley's monopoly come to an end. The two men had long enjoyed enormous financial profits and political closeness with law enforcers, as well as contracts to supply beef to Army posts and Indian reservations. On the other hand, John Tunstall had also made some enemies by becoming a partner with John Chisum, an unpopular cattleman, and Alexander McSween, a lawyer. By the time Billy the Kid came to work for John Tunstall, the situation was ominously near a breaking point.

In the fall of 1877, Dolan and Riley sent sheriff William Brady to seize horses from John Tunstall as payment for a trumped-up debt. A posse approached Tunstall, Billy, and other ranch hands. Billy and the others fled, leaving Tunstall alone to face off the posse. He was promptly shot in the head by William Morton. He was shot again in the chest, and Morton bashed his head in with his rifle butt. It was the cold-blooded murder of John Tunstall that would trigger the Lincoln County War.

Billy joined a posse of friends and employees of John Tunstall to find his killer and exact revenge. They found William Morton and Frank Baker near Rio Penasco, and after a running gun battle, the two men surrendered. Morton and Baker had been promised that they would be returned alive. Three days into their trip back to Lincoln, Billy and another man killed both prisoners, along with a member of their own posse who objected to the shootings.

Although Billy was wanted for their murders, he returned to Lincoln. Isolated, but related incidents of violence, kept the feud alive. On April 1, 1878, Sheriff Brady and two other men were walking down the main street. Billy and his friends opened fire, killing the sheriff instantly and mortally wounding one of the other men. Surprisingly, Billy stayed in Lincoln, hiding out with the help of supportive townspeople. One account relates that during a house search, Billy hid, crouched inside a barrel, while a Mexican housewife made tortillas on the barrel's lid.

By July 1878, Lincoln was a ticking time bomb. Billy and the others holed up inside the home of attorney Alexander McSween, John Tunstall's business partner. Mrs. McSween played the piano, accompanied by a servant who played the violin, while members of the two factions fired at each other. After three days however, the battle grew more intense. On the fifth day, soldiers arrived from nearby Fort Stanton to put an end to the violence. While negotiating a surrender from Billy and the McSween men, new Lincoln Sheriff George Peppin's men set fire to the wooden doors and window frames of Alexander McSween's adobe home. The fire slowly worked through to consume the floors and furniture inside. The piano was moved from room to room as the fire spread. Mrs. McSween ran from the house and was unharmed. Billy and two others sprinted out of the flaming house and got away while Alexander McSween, who refused to use a gun during the siege because it would invalidate his $10,000 life insurance policy, was not so lucky. Holding his Bible in his hand, he went outside and was met with a hail of bullets.

The Lincoln County War was over.

Billy was now a fugitive with several more murder warrants against him. But things were looking up for him as former Union General Lew Wallace was appointed territorial governor in the fall of 1878. The violence and wanton murder had gained the territory an unsavory national reputation and President Rutherford Hayes hoped the new governor could end it. Governor Wallace promised to grant amnesty to anyone who would testify against others in the Lincoln County War.

In the fall of 1880, Patrick Garrett was elected sheriff of Lincoln County. He tracked Billy and, after a gun battle, arrested him at a place called Stinking Springs. He was jailed briefly in Las Vegas, New Mexico, then in Santa Fe. He wrote repeatedly to Governor Wallace begging him to uphold his promise of amnesty, but Wallace was preoccupied with writing *Ben Hur*, the book that would bring him greater fame.

Billy was sent south to Mesilla for his trial. The April 1881 court proceedings were brief. Billy the Kid was convicted of killing Sheriff Brady and sentenced to hang in May. One source claims that the judge pronounced that he hang by the neck until "you are dead, dead, dead." Billy replied, "You can all go to hell, hell, hell." He was transferred to Lincoln, the scene of the crime.

Ironically, Billy was jailed in the upstairs of the general store owned by Dolan and Murphy. It was feared that the town jail would not be substantial enough to hold such a notorious criminal. While Sheriff Pat Garrett was away securing the materials needed to build the gallows, Billy seized an opportunity to escape.

On April 28, Deputy Robert Olinger was escorting other inmates to the restaurant across the street. According to several sources, Billy asked to be taken to the privy. On the way back, he slipped out of his handcuffs and shot Deputy J.W. Bell dead, with either Bell's own gun or one thought to have been placed in the outhouse by a sympathizer. Deputy Olinger was alarmed by the gunshots and ran back across the street. Billy then grabbed a shotgun and pointed it at the deputy. Some sources claim that, as a bystander warned out that Deputy Bell had been killed by the Kid, Olinger gasped, "And me too!" before falling to the ground dead from multiple shotgun blasts.

Billy stayed at the jail for an hour, laughing and dancing on the balcony, shouting at people who watched in horror. He stole a horse, running over the body of Deputy Olinger on his way out of town.

Now, even Governor Wallace was worried. Billy was known to have threatened to kill him for ignoring his letters. Wallace had been to Lincoln to see the site of the Lincoln County War. Traveling, as ever, with his writing materials, his wife insisted that writing at night with the a lit lamp created too tempting a target for the outlaw.

Once again, Sheriff Pat Garrett was on a manhunt for the murderer. In July 1881, Garrett went to the home of Pete Maxwell near the town of Ft. Sumner. He had received a tip that Billy was nearby, not knowing that he was actually staying in a building at Maxwell's ranch. Just after midnight, Sheriff Garrett left two deputies outside Maxwell's home and went inside his bedroom to awaken Maxwell. Garrett was sitting on Maxwell's bed while outside, Billy made his way in the darkness to Maxwell's home, barefoot and looking for something to eat. He was startled by the shadows of the deputies, and slipped inside the house. Inside Maxwell's bedroom, he did not see Pat Garrett in the darkness. According to Garrett's account, Billy asked quietly, "Who are they, Pete?"

Maxwell whispered to Garrett, "That's him."

"Quien es? Quien es?" [Who's that?] Billy asked as he ran toward the door. Garrett pulled his Colt revolver and shot him, then jumped from the bed and fired again. The startled Pete Maxwell jumped from his bed and ran for the door as Garrett shouted at the men outside not to shoot.

Billy had a large knife in his hand, and some dispute the claim from Garrett that he had a gun in the other hand. At the age of 21, Billy the Kid was dead.

Garrett's account was written in "An Authentic Life of Billy the Kid, the Noted Desperado of the Southwest." He wrote that he saw Billy's body buried the next day near Ft. Sumner, New Mexico. A newspaper article written in the *Las Vegas Daily Optic* claimed that his body was exhumed shortly after his death so that the skeleton could be cleaned and wired together for display. The story further claimed that the *Optic* was in possession of Billy's severed trigger finger.

Alabama native Pat Garrett was 31 when he killed the notorious outlaw. Although there was a $500 reward for anyone who captured Billy, Garrett had to hire a lawyer to collect the money. He ran for sheriff in Chaves County, but was defeated, then went to Uvalde, Texas and was elected County Commissioner. After that, he returned to Dona Ana County, New Mexico, where he was later elected sheriff. He was appointed by President Roosevelt as collector of customs in El Paso, and finally returned to Dona Ana County to become a rancher when the president would not reappoint him.

Ironically, accounts differ regarding the final chapter of Sheriff Pat Garrett's life. According to one, he owned a ranch that was leased to Wayne Brazel, who ran a herd of goats on Garrett's property. Garrett was in the process of selling the land, and was in a dispute with Brazel, who refused to move his goats.

On either February 29 or March 1, 1908, Carl Adamson, one of the prospective buyers, was traveling in a buckboard with Garrett looking at his property. Wayne Brazel met up with them on horseback. Garrett and Brazel argued briefly. Adamson and Garrett stepped off the buckboard to relieve themselves, and Brazel shot Garrett in the back of the head. Garrett fell to the ground and Brazel shot him again in the stomach. Pat Garrett, husband and father of nine children, was dead at the age of 57. He was buried in Las Cruces, New Mexico.

Wayne Brazel went to Las Cruces and turned himself in. Surprisingly, Brazel was acquitted of murder, claiming he fired in self-defense. An incredibly inept prosecution and the fuzzy testimony of the eyewitness caused many people to believe that Garrett's death was a conspiracy, and that perhaps Brazel was a hired assassin or took the blame for someone else who was at the scene.

The phenomena surrounding Billy the Kid continues to grow. At least two sites claim to contain his grave, and at one of them, the headstone has been chained to the ground and surrounded by a fence because it has been repeatedly stolen. Many people justify his actions by explaining that he only killed when his own life was in danger. Some see him as a representative of the oppressed, who stood up against the store monopoly and the lawmen who watched as they ran fast and loose with the law. Pat Garrett's reputation has not endured the same popularity, for reasons unknown.

The line between truth and legend has blended and blurred regarding the life of Billy the Kid. There have always been rumors that Billy did not die in July 1881. Some insist that Pat Garrett shot the wrong man and knowingly buried an impostor in order to collect the bounty. Several men have even claimed to be the outlaw. A totally credible claim has yet to surface.

People claiming to be descendants of Billy the Kid are seeking a pardon from the Governor of New Mexico for Billy's crime of shooting Sheriff Brady. One hundred twenty years after his death, he is still making headlines. More than 350 books, novels, stories, and movies have highlighted him. Billy has even been memorialized in songs and featured in science fiction.

Today, the town of Lincoln, New Mexico is visited by people from all over the world who come in search of the Billy the Kid mystique. Tumbleweeds gather up against the Tunstall and Dolan-Riley stores. Because it is not overrun with tourists, Lincoln still retains the Old West quality. Very little has changed in the town that an Alabama man named Pat Garrett once road into, a road that led him to share a destiny with one of the most controversial desperadoes this country has ever known.

Jacquelyn Procter Gray

I Am an American - Let Me Tell You Why

They left their ancestral homes in Scotland and England and hugged their families for the last time. They boarded crowded ships to sail to America, leaving behind everything and everyone they knew, in search of only one thing - freedom. When the long arm of oppression followed them across the ocean, they were determined to stand firm in their new home and fight. Centuries of pent up anger and outrage fueled by a fervent patriotism, combined into one thunderous voice loud enough to finally be heard by King George.

Under the new flag representing the country that would be known as the United States, my ancestors spent a bone-chilling winter with George Washington at Valley Forge, they rode with "Lighthorse" Harry Lee, they fought at Guilford County Courthouse and the Battle of Quebec. They were in the dragoons; they were privates, captains, majors, and colonels. When it was over, they were once and for all free from England, having paid the price with bloodshed, hardship, poverty, and even their lives.

I am an American. Let me tell you why.

My patriotism cannot be contained within the span of four designated days every year. When I look at the flag of my country, I see not only my Revolutionary War ancestors who fought against injustice, I also see my Civil War ancestors who stood on opposite sides at Chickamauga. They looked across the clouds of gunpowder, and heard the agonizing cries of men who would not live to see another beautiful sunset. They saw in each other's eyes the same dreams of independence, and a willingness to fight to the death for what they believed in.

My grandfather's grandfather died at the Battle of Atlanta; others in my family tasted death at Franklin, Shiloh, Murfreesboro, and at their own homes. My flag flew again over ancestors in Cuba who heroically liberated American prisoners in the Morro Castle, and my grandfather who left home for the first time to fight in WWI.

My flag flew again over my father as a member of the Pacific Fleet Marine Forces in Okinawa during WWII. He and his brother were bound for Japan, the first wave of Marines to land there. For my flag, they expected to die, but their lives were spared by the controversial atom bomb. They came home carrying my flag, while others in my family came home wrapped in my flag.

My flag flew again over my husband, who wore Air Force blue, and my brother, who was a Marine during the Vietnam War. We Americans suffered in silence as our flag was battered and bruised, but it was not beaten. Our flag was sewn back together with a renewed patriotism, to fly higher and stronger than ever before.

My flag is the same flag that belongs to the men who suffered in the Bataan Death March, so that I may attend the church of my choice. My flag belongs to Robert Wilkie, who was shot five times during a helicopter hunter-killer raid in Vietnam, so that I may vote for the candidate of my choice. It is the flag that belongs to Ed Horton, who in the final dramatic moments of WWII, looked into the grateful eyes of emaciated prisoners held at Gunskirchen Lager and told them that they were free to go home. It is the same flag that gave comfort and hope to the men who endured horrors in prisoner-of-war camps, so that I may write my opinions without fear of imprisonment. It is the flag of the men and women who came home crippled and maimed, so that the social class I was born into will not determine the limits of my potential.

As a child of eleven, it is the same flag that was seared into my memory as it lay draped over my father's coffin, while the echoes of taps were carried heavenward on a dry dusty wind.

I am an American. *Now* you know *why*.

Bacil Procter, Stanton Procter

Cowboys, Operas, and Marines

The September 25, 1942, edition of the *Roy Record* ran the following headline: "Roy Youth Enlists in Training for Leatherneck Service." The article went on to say, "Young [Bacil] Procter has punched cows on New Mexico ranges during his summer vacations, and the Roy youth wants to get in more than one good punch at the Hirohitomen!" His brother Stanton enlisted in the Marines shortly after, and they would spend nearly all of their time in service together.

The following excerpts are from letters written to them by their father, mother, sister, and a few friends. Their father, a rancher, typed his letters with his index fingers and made many typographical and spelling errors, retained here. Their mother and sister, both high school teachers, often discussed music in their letters, as all were classically trained musicians and singers. Early letters were written to them while they were training at Harvard and MIT.

"January 7, 1944 - My Dear Boys,...I wish I could tell you both how empty it is here since our boys have gone. It seems that still I should hear your dear voices, see you standing beside the stove...or many other things concerning every day life in which I have always known you...Tell us all about your work, where you stay, how you like New England, how winter is there, etc. We are having another blizzard here this morning, - wind blowing a gale, fine snow filling the air and cutting like sleet...I love you both so, and how eagerly and longingly I am looking forward to your coming home with no war calling you away again...I enjoyed your telling of your adventure in New York, but, oh my, why do they all drink? All my love, Mamma."

According to a story passed down in the family, the family named was originally spelled *Proctor*. When the Missouri clan got into a dispute over who to back during the Civil War, those family members that sympathized with the South changed the spelling of their name to *Procter*.

"Jan 13, 1944 -...I just got Your letter...with the $100.00 check, thanks very much,...one thing sure I dont want you boys to skimp in any way, I want you to stay right there on the Job and Knock them all over...I went to the meeting last night where we was orginizing to put over the Next War bond drive...Harding Co is alloted $28,300 for this drive, which isnt much. but I may think it is a lot before we sell that many...it has sure been cold here and still is. the Hot water froze in Our back room and busted

and it was a fright. I just sawed a hole in the floor and went down and plugged the holes as We dont use that room any way...I bought a little Alfalfa today. $42.00 per ton, thats high enough I think. But we have to live. the hens layed 23 eggs Yesterday. I have sold everything but 50 of the red hens...your Mother is sure planning big on coming there next summer. so we must have her go or bust a Gut...I think you are there where You can go to hear a lot of the Big Wigs. in Music and lectures also. well I will twist off...as ever Your Dad."

"Jan 19th, 1944 - My Dear Kiddoes - Mrs. Gilstrap is in Raton. in Hospital nervious break down, too much worry and too much hard work...the pig is now putting on just a little fat, town is no good place for 4 leged hogs. the train killed 8 nice shoats yesterday...Your Daddy."

Bacil and Stanton's parents had traveled in covered wagons from Missouri to homestead the high plains of eastern New Mexico. They settled in the town of Mills where money could be made growing wheat. Their three children were born there and J.B. Procter, as the town manager, advertised for folks back east to move out west and enjoy the good life. But one day the winds came, choking the air with thick dust until the skies were darker than night. The Dust Bowl Days of the 1930s parched the earth, turning the lush grasslands of the Southwest into a desolate wasteland. The only respite from the howling wind was when night finally came. The cattle and sheep died and people abandoned their ranches and dreams. Mills was never the same. The Procters left the farm and moved to Roy, a community 10 miles away.

"January 29, 1944 - My Dear Boys,…Have you heard the recent news…about the horrors of the treatment Japan gave our boys immediately following Pearl Harbor? The radio says bond sales sky-rocketed to unbelievable proportions, and Americans are crying for complete destruction of Tokyo. People here who have boys prisoners there are almost frantic and lose all reason, it is said, when the Japs are mentioned…All my love, Mamma."

"Febr 25th 1944 - Dear Kiddoes. all of Both of You…Well I just got Your letters…and will answer them before the Women comes home…I got me a Parker Pen and Pencil. cost me \$12.50…it is sure windy here today. and dust blowing…Say Roy Myers has bought the Old Wilco Hotel…and expects to tare it down…Lemer Gave me the Hen House then I gave it back to Him as it was the only Hen House worth Mooving. The preacher here is mooving to Mouniment N.M. about 12 miles from Hobbs. I may go with the truck when they moove him. and Look the situation over. it is Oil fields down there. No news except who Killed the Cat. as ever Your Old Daddy."

Bacil was named for his father, but most people insisted on spelling it *Basil*. After joining the Marines, he gave up and spelled it with an "s" as well.

"March 5, 1944 - Dear Lieutenants! Of course I don't suppose you can talk much about your work, but I am sure you would be able to tell us if you had a chance to play a Steinway grand, Basil, and put your feet on it while you read a 'western.' Stanton, I saw an advertisement in 'Life' for Ipana in which a page of your famous G major Sonata by Beethoven was pictured...We have had a unit of 250 aviation students here, but we are now down to 150...We wish there were more men, as we are particularly short on the bass section...Clara and Irving Bartley."

Bacil majored in chemistry and music, and minored in math at New Mexico Highlands University. His music teacher complained when he wore cowboy boots to his organ lessons. He worked on ranches and rode in rodeos to earn tuition money for college. At one job, his task was to saddle Gary Cooper's horse for him when he came to visit a wealthy local rancher.

"March 10th 1944 -...we are planning on going to the Show tonight. (Tumbling Weed) Come over and go with Us...the Ranch Home of Mr. Lee Yarbrough was burned about tuesday I think. You will get the dope in the Roy Record. I made the deal on the State lands...I made enough to Pay my debts and have two or three dollars besides...so lets shout for once...say You should have seen me shopping in Albuquerque. I had to get a lot of stuff. so I got me a Paper bag and shoped. Just like an old woman. I got 2

*dozen nice towls 2 dozen wash rags etc., Bobbie pins. Safety Pins.
also got me a suit. and shirt and two pr of socks and two pairs of
Underwaire...as ever Your Daddy."*

The arrival of the *Roy Record* was an eagerly anticipated
event for Bacil and Stanton. It was haphazardly printed -
once the front page was printed upside-down, and the
homespun stories of the wild west kept the other Marines in
stitches.

*"April 22, 1944 - My Dear Precious Boys,...A short wave
message came into the U.S. from somewhere that Dan (Roberts) is
alive and held prisoner. So it has recently been announced over
KFUN that the War Dept. has notified the Roberts family that he
is now a prisoner...All my love, Mamma"*

*"May 8, 1944 - My Dear Boys, Just a line this morning. to
let you know we are all about as common. also Bacil Mc they Put
into the Birth Day offering Yesterday. and they had a Nice service
for you. wish You could have been there...Sure hope this finds
You both well. and Fat...with love, Daddy"*

The brothers told the story that their father had once
written a letter to Sears Roebuck asking them to send him x-
number of rolls of toilet paper. Sears wrote back and told
him to look on a certain page of their catalog and give them
an order number. Procter wrote to Sears and said that if he
had their catalog, he wouldn't need their toilet paper.

"Nov. 28, 1944 - My Dear Boys,...Say as to using a Jeep. dont use one only enough to learn how to handle it. as too many Boys get out to haveing a good time and I have known of two or more bunches having recks and killing some of them. so dont take one out only to just learn how to handle them. I sure wish I had a new Jeep now. as I think it would be a dandy farm implement. Your old Daddy"

"Nov. 29, 1944 - My Dear Boys,...the time is going quickly for I don't want you to leave the homeland...still it doesn't seem possible that you have been gone almost 2 wks. but oh, how we miss you both! I look at your bed, your clothing, books, blue uniforms,...and almost choke. The piano, too, though it recalls you both so pleasantly, and means so much to bring you back in memory, yet there is a hushed sadness there, too...As your train left Tucumcari we drove up the highway in its 'wake' and, for 30 miles, could see the smoke billowing up to the sky. Then as it went East and we went West it vanished, and we felt as if we had said goodbye again. I told Daddy that I thought he was driving to try to overtake the train...All my love, Mamma"

A letter written on Marine Corps stationary was dated 3 December 1944:

"Dear Stanton and Bacil, You cannot imagine the deep sense of pride I felt as I passed thru New Mexico on my recent trip out there...Raton, Albuquerqe (or however you spell it) fell off my tongue with the glibness of the native...I noticed that the two of

71

you were still together, as of last month…Do you still play pitch as often as you used to? Remember our partner in the Up and Down the River escapades?…Well, he's out here in the Air Warning squadron…Now look - I want an answer to this letter. Don't stick it in that drawer where you have all the rest strewn. Answer it, and then throw it away. As ever, Ken"

"December 6, 1944 - My Dear Boys, In Floersheim's window are pictures of the boys who have gone from Harding Co. I think…that the Procter Lieutenants are the finest looking. Your picture is surely an advertisement too, for the Fabian Bachrack Portrait Co…Tuffy is still the homely watch dog about the place. I think he stands and looks for you boys, waiting to bite your feet. All my love, Mamma"

Their mother commented that she was unhappy with the addition of "Marine Fighter Squadron" in their new address.

"December 14, 1944 - My Dear Precious Boys, Mr. John Weisdorfer received a telegram a few days ago from Washington D.C. stating that a boy from Oklahoma had made a broadcast from Japs and in his remarks said that Lawrence Weisdorfer was well and all right…I saw Mrs. Wester. Her hair is snow white. She said that, though the Navy Dept. sent her George's personal belongings they tell her that they have not given up hope, and think it quite possible that the men are on one of the islands in the

Northern waters, and will later be rescued...All my love, Mamma"

Lawrence Weisdorfer survived the Bataan Death March, despite having a nail driven through his skull. However, the trauma he suffered continued to simmer slowly inside him, long after he came home.

George Wester was one of six brothers who enlisted to fight. He was on the maiden voyage of a U.S. submarine when it surfaced among Japanese warships. His body was never recovered. His mother blamed herself for his death because George was underage, and she had signed for him to enlist.

"December 17, 1944 - My Dear Boys, This afternoon we listened to Bro. Fuller at 5 P.M., as they sang 'All Because of Calvary' I remember how you have loved it so long, Stanty,...The sun was low in the west and the sunset was golden everywhere, all so quiet...Well since this sounds rather broken and without continuity of thought (as Mark Twain said about Webster's Dictionary) I will say good night and may God keep and bless my boys, ever - even to Eternity's portal. All my love, Mamma"

Stanton accused Bacil of being unsociable because he would disappear every night as the Marines gathered to swap stories and play cards. On Christmas morning, he discovered why. On Stanton's rack was a homemade hand-tooled leather wallet and a hand-carved wooden jewelry box.

"December 18, 1944 - My Dearest Brothers,...the Navy hasn't given George (Wester) up definitely, and John (Wester) is in England..."

George Wester's brother John was a bombardier for the Army Air Corps. While stationed in England, he went into a pub one night. Not knowing the conversion rate from American to English currency, he handed an unknown amount of money to the barman, trusting him to make correct change for the drinks he ordered. An Englishman watched this exchange a few times, then asked the bartender why he was handing John more money in change than John was giving him for his drinks. "Because the Yanks aren't afraid to bomb in the daytime," he said. "and this is my way of helping the Americans."

"December 25, 1944 - My Dear Precious Boys,...hearing your dear voices this morning gave inspiration, hope, courage, and an added vitality which were much enjoyed by us all. Even the Roy operator expressed her happiness at your calling home...As we sat down to the breakfast table on the morning of Christmas Eve, all of us had the same thought, - the 2 empty places. None of us could eat. I left the table to stop the tears, Daddy went to the bathroom to be alone, and (your sister) sat

alone at the table with bowed head. However, we had first offered thanks and asked God's care upon you boys...I do know how empty your places are in the home, though in our hearts you are ever with us and before us...Roy Self said that Saturday night the Japs persuaded our prisoner boys to sing 'Holy Night' and 'O, Come All ye Faithful,' over the radio short wave. He said we have never heard such expression and meaning as the boys gave in their voices from Japan. How my heart goes out to the boys in prison camps as well as to all others in service...Lovingly, Mama"

"December 30, 1944 - My Dear Boys, Well, the year is rapidly drawing to a close, and we shall have a new page for our deeds to be recorded, in a few hours...As this is probably my last letter this year, Boys, again let me assure of the happiness you have given us this year, and all the years of your lives...All my love, Mamma"

"Sunday Jan. 7th 1945 - My Dear Boys,...I never can think of any news when I get ready to write. But will say. I am making a nice little tralor. one that will do to go fishing and hunting in if we ever want to go. I have turned the Axle over so it will go over a rock at least 12 inches high...Charles boy come home christmas on Furlow. and he went twice with Toms girl. they kicked up a chunk I guess and got married...they went one night at 2 O.Clock and got their lisence and got the Methodest preacher up at 3 O.Clock

and got married. I guess she was afraid to wait until He sobered up dont you. as ever Your Daddy."

J.B. Procter was one of the last of the cowboys of the Wild West. His grandson once asked if he could get a rattlesnake for him to take to school for his science project. His grandson failed to specify dead or alive, so J.B. caught a live one for him.

"February 10, 1945 - My Dear Boys,...A few days ago the news said that Japan says America is very unsportsmanlike in the way we are so mercilessly attacking their cities...Our church has a new service flag now, a beautiful thing. Red, white, and blue silk, your names all embroidered in blue silk with a blue star beside each name, on white silk ground, bordered with a wide red silk edge...Daddy says he will see to your (livestock) brand at Albuquerque for we can't find the certificate...Lovingly, Mama"

In a letter dated February 15, 1945, they learned that the parents of their college friend, Dan Roberts, had reconciled themselves that he was no longer alive.

An alumni newsletter from New Mexico Highlands University announced: "...Sorrow blanketed the campus recently with arrival of the news of the death of Capt. Dan Roberts, who was killed in New Guinea after having brought down 14 Jap Zeros. His score was the second best in that theater, where he had been on duty as pilot of a P-38

for approximately 22 months. The official announcement
said that he was killed in action over Alexishafen, New
Guinea, on Nov. 9. Dan's death brings to seven the number
of Highlands alumni, all officers, who have given their lives
in the service of their country..."

*"February 23, 1945 - My Dear Dear Boys, Somehow as I
hear of the staggering losses of Marines on Iwo Jima, I shudder
and feel so reverent in my thanks to our God that He has you boys
where you are...Daddy is out to the farm. I think the
Government Agency is beginning on the lake today - draining it,
terracing, etc. Four and one-half dollars per hour, plus board and
room sounds like lucrative employment, doesn't it? Daddy is so
anxious to get cows again. He now has 1 cow, 1 heifer, and 2
steers...Lovingly, Mama"*

*"March 9, 1945 - My Dear Dear Boys, I cannot get myself
quite calm or happy tonight since knowing that my boys may be
separated. I am praying that you may not (?) if it would be God's
will that you may remain together...I am putting out the
gladiolas...put up a wire fence to keep Frank's 4 old hens out of
them. His flock has neither increased nor decreased for 2 or 3
years, they are permanently fixed in number...Lovingly, Mama"*

*"March 28, 1945 - Dear Stanton,...I think Your Mama is
planning on going to Springer Sunday. But I have an Idea Ill
stay here. as I dont care about seeing My Old friend You know
who...I feel sure that they will soon be sending You and (Bacil)*

*across. so where ever you go or what ever befalls You. Just
remember we will be here waiting for the Day…I had a letter from
Kenneth. He is in the Philippines. and Roy said his Boy Ben. is at
or on way to Iwa Jima. I sure hope he made it through that
struggle…as Ever Your Daddy"*

Basil knew that the Japanese left booby traps for
Americans looking to bring a souvenir home to America.
He wanted to pick up a Japanese helmet, but knowing it
might kill him to pick it up, he lassoed it, cowboy-style, and
dragged it behind him for some time until he decided it was
safe to pick it up.

*"8 May 1945 - Dear Stupid and Ugly: Tonight while looking
through some of the men's record books I came across the
unbelievable. I found a fellow who was born in Roy, New Mexico
and not ashamed to admit it…he says that your pop and his pop
are buddy, buddy…I think you people owe me a letter but because
I happen to have the duty tonight…I might as well waste part of
the night writing to you morons…I've lost track of most of the
radar men floating around the country…If you ever get in this
neck of the woods don't forget to look us up. Rheta says its been a
long time since last she saw such ugliness but she thinks she can
look at one of you at the time without becoming ghastly sick…Lt.
Albert Pinsky"*

*"Dear Stanty, Went out on Bull Head today to put up
strafing targets. Had a good time. A little excitement once when*

some navy bombers came over, didn't see us, and dropped 5 practice bombs less than 100 yds from where we were working...Be good B[acil] P.S. If you want an extra good record get 'Intermezzo' from 'Cavalleria Rusticana' - one of the prettiest I ever heard."

After spending time on Okinawa, Captains Basil and Stanton Procter were given orders to join the first wave of Marines headed to Japan for the invasion. Before they could leave, America dropped atomic bombs on Hiroshima and Nagasaki, saving the lives of these two men and thousands and thousands more. After the war, Basil married Peggy Hundley, a girl from Limestone County, Alabama and went back to Roy, New Mexico. Stanton married Berta Davis, a Roy girl. Both had families and became college professors.

On December 31, 1968, Stanton Procter died of a brain hemorrhage. He was 47. Nearly nine months later, at the age of 51, his brother Basil died of a heart attack.

A sorrowful wind lifts dust from foundation ruins of the ghost town of Mills. Only the clackety-clack of old windmill blades breaks the lonely silence where once there was life and laughter. Two brothers, who walked and fought side-by-side in life, now rest side-by-side in the ghost town graveyard.

Robert Donnell - A Man of the Ages

Robert Donnell must have had an amazing amount of faith. The family property was destroyed by the British at the Battle of Guilford County Courthouse in North Carolina. Their possessions were later burned by Indians at Nickajack in the Tennessee wilderness. Any normal man would have become embittered, but Donnell knew his purpose early in life and his conviction never wavered. He came to the wilderness now known as Alabama, fell in love with the people and the land, and left an imprint that will not soon be forgotten. As a minister for a time at the Mooresville, Alabama brick church, Donnell caused a furor with the residents of the community that caused one man to angrily swear to tear out the bricks with his own hands if Donnell refused to vacate the pulpit.

Robert Donnell was born in about 1784. His parents were members of the Nottingham Colony that left York County, Pennsylvania to settle in North Carolina in 1753. His father farmed in Guilford County, North Carolina when the Revolutionary War upended their lives. The Battle of Guilford County Courthouse destroyed his property, but he fought to protect his family and home as a private in the North Carolina militia. For serving under Nathaniel Greene, the British placed a bounty on his head in the amount of 200 pounds.

After the Revolution, the family migrated to Wilson County, Tennessee, and watched helplessly as hostile Indians burned what little they had left of their possessions, as they floated down the Tennessee River on a flatboat. To compound the family's troubles, Robert's father died of fever in 1798, leaving the 15-year-old young man as sole support for his mother and four sisters.

Robert inherited an endurance that was forged by centuries of ancestors who knew nothing but a harsh and violent life. He was a direct descendant of Alexander XII, Chief of the MacDonald Clan in the Highlands of Scotland. Recognized as mighty warriors, earlier MacDonalds earned the privilege of fighting at the immediate right of Scotland's King Robert the Bruce, who took up the cause of Scotland's obstinate desire for independence from England after the vicious murder of Scotsman William Wallace in the 12th century.

A particularly dark event in history that took place over 300 years ago, is still felt by the MacDonald descendants to this day. England's King William ordered that all clan chiefs travel to Inverary to take an oath of allegiance to him before January 1, 1692, with the understanding that all members of each clan could then enjoy the promised protection of the king. The chief of the MacDonald clan left Glencoe for Inverary, but was delayed by a snowstorm. When he arrived, he found that the magistrate was gone for several days. Finally, on January 6 the clan chief took the oath to the king.

The king seized this opportunity as an excuse to make an example of the MacDonald clan by having them annihilated. He sent his regiment which included many members of the Campbell Clan to Glencoe with this secret message, "You are hereby ordered to fall upon the rebels, the MacDonalds of Glencoe, and to put all to the sword under seventy."

For two weeks, the visiting regiment enjoyed the hospitality of the MacDonalds, eating their food and sleeping in their homes. Although the MacDonalds shared an alarming sense of unease about the situation, their clan chief chastised them for suspecting the very men who were sworn to protect them.

In the pre-dawn hours of February 13, 1692, the regiment arose and carried out the blood bath, slaughtering their hosts and families in a tragedy that became known as the Glencoe Massacre. The white swirling snow fell upon the bloodied bodies of those who were cut down as they tried to run, while the wind carried their death cries into the cold darkness.

The spectacular beauty of Glencoe would forever be stained with the blood of betrayal, and cement the centuries-old feud between the Campbells and the MacDonalds.

John Dalrymple, Master of Stair, was given credit for organizing the attack. The Dalrymple coat-of-arms contains nine lozenges, and because of that, the nine of diamonds card is today known as the "Curse of Scotland."

Alexander's son had already left Scotland, lived in Ireland, and then came to America when he received news of the massacre. For whatever reason he had to leave Scotland, life for his descendants would not be any easier.

The spelling of MacDonald has many variations. According to Donnell descendants in Wilson County, Tennessee, there was, at some point, a schism in the family that caused one branch to alter the family name.

The death of Robert Donnell's father in 1798 encumbered him at an early age and no doubt prepared him for the future he embraced. It was said that he could split more rails than any grown man around and that he built the first grist mill in the area of Wilson County, Tennessee where the family settled. Although he lacked a formal education, his mother may have taught him to read after daily chores were finished. He read and re-read the Bible he carried as he walked behind the plow, and it was on one of these days that he experienced the epiphany that would change his life.

In the year 1800, American churches experienced what became known as the Great Revival, an intense effort to bring Christianity to every household. Although it was at first sanctioned by most of the organized religions of that time, it fueled a religious frenzy that alarmed those who promoted it in the first place. The Great Revival began in 1797 with fasting and prayer, and a nation-wide outpouring of the Holy Spirit. However, sensational evangelists began decrying the old ideas and accusing many established churches of having a godless ministry with unconverted ministers in the pulpit. An inevitable split was created in many churches.

For Americans of that time, the church was an all-important part of their lives. Long before the modern distractions, the church provided a social outlet as well as a place for repentance. The minister was a leader in the community. The wilderness colonies that did not have a full-time minister, had to wait as much as three months for their circuit-riding preacher to come around to perform wedding ceremonies and after-the-fact funeral services.

The Presbyterian Church cautiously endorsed the Great Revival at first, but time and again, attention was called to an especially fervent pocket of Presbyterians who lived in the Cumberland region of Tennessee and Kentucky. Even before the church was organized, they were referred to as "those *Cumberland* Presbyterians." When the new church was officially formed in 1810, they simply formalized the name.

Robert Donnell was converted during this time of religious fervor, and although he felt the call to preach, his lack of education was an obstacle. He prayed for some sort of opening, and the guidelines of the newly formed Cumberland Presbyterian Church provided that opportunity for him.

The first Cumberland Presbyterian ministers, which included Robert Donnell, were dismissed by ministers of other faiths who were generally older, educated in the classics, and owned finer clothing. These early C.P. ministers often swam the rivers wearing homespun clothing made by their mothers or wives to come to the newly-settled frontiers in this area. They slept on the ground or if lucky, on the floors of settlers' homes. In this area of the country, they had little competition with other ministers, who felt that their education entitled them to permanent churches, a steady income, and more affluent church members.

In his book, "The History of the Cumberland Presbyterian Church" published in 1888, B.W. McDonnold quoted a man who said, "The first generation of Cumberland Presbyterians were the most intensely spiritual people that I have ever known...Those people lived nearer heaven than ordinary Christians do now." Their young ministers were described as "flaming fires" and their converts to Christianity were many in number.

Robert Donnell held the first camp meeting in the new settlement of Huntsville, Alabama and is credited with starting many churches in North Alabama that still stand today. As a moving force in that area's religious life, he arrived so soon after the settlers, that several churches were founded as the land was being cleared for the very first crop.

It was customary in those days for a young minister to travel with an older minister, for the purpose of fostering the education of the young man and assessing his qualities as a future leader in the church. They discussed lessons, doctrine, and the Bible during the many hours they traveled together. Rev. Donnell had a special cane that contained an inkwell in the top so that he could ride horseback and record his thoughts at the same time.

Life for early settlers in this territory was dangerous as they tried to co-exist with sometimes hostile Indians. He and his cousin Rev. Robert Bell were among the missionaries who helped educate and convert many Chickasaw Indians in what is now the state of Mississippi, to Christianity. In 1815, he went to work as a missionary to the Cherokees in East Tennessee.

Though Donnell was immersed in the religious life of this area, exhibiting what has been described as an astounding endurance, he spent much time traveling in search of more converts. In 1817, he was in Jackson County, Tennessee conducting a camp meeting when he was invited to stay at the home of James Webb Smith, a wealthy plantation owner. Donnell met and fell in love with Smith's daughter Ann Eliza, and they were married in March, 1818.

Robert and Ann Eliza enjoyed a happy marriage as they settled into life in this exciting time if Alabama's history. Their bliss was marked with extreme tragedy, as they suffered the devastating loss of four of their five children in the next few years. Donnell was traveling through North Alabama when he received word that his daughter died in Tennessee at the home of his father-in-law. His hand trembled in grief as he wrote through eyes clouded by tears to his beloved Ann Eliza, "My wife must weep alone while I am trying to comfort other bereaved mothers." After only 10 short years of marriage, death claimed the frail Ann Eliza at the age of 32.

A few years later, Robert Donnell was visiting Reverend Dr. Jacob Lindley in Ohio, when he made Donnell promise to look in on his daughter who was a teacher in Lawrence County, Alabama. The meeting was arranged, they fell in love, and in 1832, Donnell married Clarissa Lindley. Although they had no children together, what emptiness they may have felt was filled in later years with the laughter of the many children of Donnell's only surviving child, James Webb Smith Donnell.

Donnell's influence as a dynamic minister was not without controversy, however. The Mooresville, Alabama brick church, which still stands, was built in the early 1800's as a community church. The understanding was that each year, a new minister would occupy the pulpit, representing a different denomination. When Robert Donnell came in 1835 as a Cumberland Presbyterian minister, he amassed an immediate following, and at the conclusion of his year in the pulpit, he refused to give up the church. An angry outlash by residents was not enough to force him out. One of the men who helped build the historic church threatened to pull the bricks out with his bare hands. In the end, the foothold established by the Cumberland Presbyterians prevailed.

Rev. Donnell grappled with the moral aspects of slavery his entire life. Although he grew up knowing hard work and hardship, he inadvertently became a slave-owner as a result of his marriage to his first wife, Ann Eliza. By Alabama law, he was prevented from freeing his slaves, and although he offered to pay for their passage to Liberia, they would not go. He turned down the chance to pastor a church in Memphis because he would not take his slaves so far from their families on neighboring farms. Donnell prayed to God for answers to this situation. He called the slaves into his dining room twice daily for prayer, and tolerated his overseer as he chastised him for keeping them from their work. Donnell informed him that his concern was for their souls, first and foremost.

By 1851, Donnell's house in Athens was completed, and he and Clarissa settled into a comfortable and pleasant life together. While conducting an outdoor camp meeting near Huntsville in 1853, Donnell became ill. At first he shrugged his illness off, but over the next few months, his condition worsened until his death in 1855.

His good friend, Rev. Thomas Calhoun, preached the funeral sermon. As the mourners gathered, an ominous thunder cloud approached carrying with it, torrents of rain. Calhoun raised his arms heavenward and in a pleading, yet commanding voice, he asked God not to let the rain disturb their worship. The scene was remembered and retold for years to come. A drenching downpour accompanied by thunder and bolts of lightning swept swiftly toward the huddled crowd. Hard rain fell all around the crowd, but the mourners, as well as their tethered horses nearby, remained dry. Those who witnessed it felt that it had to be a tribute to the man who devoted his life to God.

The Civil War arrived with death, destruction, and the end of slavery. Donnell's son and his family lived in the

Athens home when Yankee soldiers camped around it during the Union occupation of Athens. One soldier complained that someone in the house emptied a chamber pot from the second story window onto their campfire, destroying their supper.

With the enthusiasm of their new freedom after the war, former slaves of the Cumberland Presbyterians formed their own denomination, now called the Cumberland Presbyterian Church of America. The national headquarters of this historic denomination is in Huntsville, Alabama. Because the histories of the two churches have parallel paths, they still maintain and enjoy a connection today.

Long-time curator of the Donnell home, Faye Axford, is herself a distinguished historian who has thoroughly researched and written about Rev. Robert Donnell as well as Limestone County. The Donnell home was condemned in the 1970s and doomed to the wrecking ball. Fortunately, concerned Athens, Alabama citizens saved it from destruction, and it is now open for tours.

In 1906, a crushing blow was dealt by the national General Assembly of the Cumberland Presbyterian Church when it ordered that all Cumberland Presbyterian churches unite with the Presbyterian U.S.A. Church. Many worshipers arrived on Sunday morning to find a padlock on their church doors, along with the notice that it was now the property of the Presbyterian Church. Approximately one third of the former Cumberland Presbyterians obeyed the order, another third of the churches simply ceased to exist, and the remaining members rolled up their sleeves and began rebuilding new churches, and continued calling themselves Cumberland Presbyterian in defiance of the order. There are many Presbyterian churches of both denominations in this area, that were founded by Rev. Robert Donnell.

After his death, schools in Madison County, Alabama and Winchester, Tennessee were named for Robert Donnell. Surely, Robert Donnell would be proud to know that nearly 150 years after his death, the presbytery which governs several churches in North Alabama, was named in his honor.

An Angry Woman With a Hatchet

Carrie Nation was angry, and she made sure everyone knew it. Her visit to Alabama in October 1902 brought the curious and the righteous to the Huntsville Depot. They had to witness firsthand the zealot known for her excoriating insults and destructive outbursts. At nearly 6' tall and 180 pounds, the hatchet slinging woman dressed in black cut a formidable figure, making the genteel Huntsville people shudder in fright.

Carrie Nation made a reputation for herself as a crusader against the evils of drink, but as her following grew, she supported the women's suffrage movement and attacked those who indulged in the use of tobacco. Not even the Masonic Lodge escaped her wrath. She was bitter over the failure of her two marriages, and it seemed that everyone was to blame, everyone that is, except Carrie Nation.

Carrie was born in Kentucky in 1846. During the Civil War, she worked in a hospital in Independence, Missouri, caring for the wounded in both gray and blue. Her first husband, a physician, was an alcoholic. She left him just after the birth of her only child, a daughter. Within six months, her husband was dead. She blamed alcohol and the Masonic Lodge. According to her, his lodge brothers encouraged him to drink and stay away from home. It was a stretch, but it cleared her conscience.

Carrie, her mother-in-law, and her baby daughter lived together in a small house, and Carrie became a school teacher. In her autobiography, she claimed that she was fired for instructing the children to pronounce "a" in a title incorrectly. After her dismissal, she prayed to God to send her a husband to support her family. Ten days after her prayer, she met David Nation, a Union veteran who was a lawyer, minister, and editor. Her friends cautioned her against marrying a man 19 years her senior, but a few weeks later, they exchanged vows.

It was a miserable marriage.

She blamed her husband for their unhappy marriage and said that for the rest of her life, she envied women who had husbands that loved them. She later reasoned that her success in the temperance movement would have been impossible had she been happily married. Perhaps her husband did not like the fact that she accused him of not being saved in the church, and not being "called" to the ministry. Maybe he didn't appreciate that she wrote his sermons for him, constantly railing against alcohol and tobacco. Surely he objected because she sat on the front row as he delivered his sermons, instructing him to raise or lower his voice, speak faster or slower. Most assuredly he blanched when she stood in the aisle and told him it was time to end his sermon. If he continued to preach, he might have been embarrassed when she marched up to the pulpit, shut his Bible, handed him his hat, and told him to go home.

Only Carrie was surprised when David Nation was asked to resign as minister. When members of the church asked her to quit attending because she continued to be disruptive, she defiantly attended anyway. But Carrie was about to find her own calling.

The Women's Christian Temperance Union was established in the early 1880s and the membership quickly grew in number. They were already a strong force at the time the convention was held in Huntsville, Alabama in November 1895, seven years before Carrie's visit. The convention attendees discussed, at length, the use of unfermented sacramental wine in church. A presentation was given about the number of colleges that came to regret admitting students who smoked cigarettes. A telegram was sent by Mrs. McBryde, who was re-elected as vice president, but unable to attend. It said simply, "First Corinthians, fifteenth and fifty-eighth." (*Therefore, my beloved brethren, be ye steadfast, unmoveable, always abounding in the work of the Lord, forasmuch as ye know that your labour is not in vain in the Lord.*) Though not especially imaginative, the motto of the WCTU was "For God and Home and Native Land."

It was only natural that the Women's Christian Temperance Union and Carrie Nation would find each other.

In her hometown of Medicine Lodge, Kansas, Carrie's cause began to take on undertones of violence and fanaticism. One day in 1899, she and another woman prayed against the evils of drink. They marched to Mort Strong's saloon, gathering a crowd as they went. Carrie began a tirade. When she tried to go in, Mr. Strong met her and physically escorted her out. It was just the beginning. With much persistence, she succeeded in getting his business closed down, along with several other saloons in town. She then raised her hatchet to a bar in Kiowa, and took on the Hotel Carey in Wichita, one of the poshest establishments around.

During her many rallies, she spoke of the great joy of saloon-smashing, accusing her opponents of being "rum-soaked, whiskey-swilled, saturnine-faced rummies." She encouraged women to take up rocks, hatchets, and brickbats and experience the great joy of promoting moral righteousness through the destruction of drinking houses.

Carrie was a celebrity by the time she made her journey to Huntsville. Even ladies who were not members of the Women's Christian Temperance Union came to the train depot to see what kind of spectacle the woman who wore masculine-looking clothing, hat, and shoes would produce. Men, women, and children crowded the platform to see her and hear what she had to say. They were surprised and appalled when Carrie turned on them. Peering inside one carriage, she shouted, "You ought to go home and tear off those plumes and gew gaws and make corns on your knees praying for your lost soul. You are lost, sister, lost! Pray God for repentance!" She waved her hatchet for dramatic effect, and those who could turn their carriages around, quickly left.

Carrie's trip to Huntsville included a speech at the opera house and a visit to several Huntsville drinking establishments, including the Dew Drop. She then went to C. C. Baxter's saloon and singled out a young man just about to take a drink. Caught between the devil and the deep blue sea, he was forced to endure her scorching tirade. The crowd grew until it included, not only the women of town, but several hundred men and boys. Accommodations in Huntsville could not be found at a hotel that did not have a bar, so she stayed at Mrs. Turner's home on Randolph Street. When she got back on the train, the Women's Christian Temperance Union basked in a surge of renewed faith, and the saloon owners let out a great sigh of relief.

Her influence in Huntsville was ultimately successful. The saloons were eventually closed by a combination of "prejudice, politics, and petticoats."

Carrie became consumed with her crusade. By fighting against the legalization of alcohol, she found a niche that gained her fame and, unfortunately, another failed marriage. Her husband finally sued her for divorce after 24 years of marriage. She fought the divorce, although she admitted she did not plan to live with her husband again. She received much criticism for having failed at marriage. After a lifetime of judging others, the time had come for her to get a taste of her own medicine.

Carrie moved to the Oklahoma Territory in 1905 to fight for a dry constitution in the land that, in 1907, would become the 46th state. She received many hatchets and weapons as gifts which are now on display, along with remnants of smashed saloons, at the Kansas State Historical Society. She boasted that she had been arrested 30 times between 1900 and 1910 for her protests on prohibition. Carrie Nation died in Washington, D.C. on June 9, 1911.

Today, history remembers Carrie Nation as a Bible carrying zealot who funneled her bitterness into controversial causes of the day. At least two establishments have chosen to honor her, albeit in a tongue-in-cheek manner. In Los Gatos, California, her name appears on the frosted glass door of a high-end bar. Under the letters, "Carrie Nation's Bar" are crossed hatchets.

And so her legacy has turned into a mockery of the very ideals she promoted. Perhaps if she had known the love of a good man, the world would have never heard of a woman named Carrie Nation.

The Bells of Angelus

Staff Sergeant Odell Dobson regained consciousness and rolled out of the flaming B-24 as it plummeted toward the earth. He pulled the cord on his parachute and the white silk ballooned up and unfurled, yanking him up to drift in the cold air. As he floated down, the formation of Liberators moved away from him. He watched as American and German planes fell from the sky, some spinning, one tumbling end over end, as they hurtled to the earth in fiery balls of flame.

The flight moved on and disappeared in the haze of the distance. The fighters followed, taking with them the horrendous sounds of air combat. Plumes of smoke arose from wreckages on the ground as Dobson gently floated down into the surreal serenity below him now.

Bong! Bong! Bong! From the German village below, he heard the church bells peal the noon Angelus service.

Bong! Bong! Bong! He looked down to see an old man following a plow pulled by an ox, while a woman switched the animal.

101

Bong! Bong! Bong! With the use of only one eye, Dobson saw that his left flight boot was gone and blood was pouring across his foot.

Villagers peered upwards and watched his slow descent as they walked onto the field to wait. Nine more bells tolled the end of the church service. Dobson was sure he would land right on top of the farmer's ox. Instead, with an abrupt jolt, he landed in a nearby freshly plowed field. As quickly as possible, he unhooked and crawled from the parachute harness and started to run. Three times he stumbled and fell, then realized he had been seriously wounded in both legs. Carrying pitchforks and gasoline, the villagers closed in on him.

Odell Dobson was a high schooler in Schoolfield, Virginia when the Japanese bombed Pearl Harbor. After his graduation in 1942, he went to enlist in the Army Air Corps pilot training program. To his great disappointment, he washed out after ten hours of dual flight training, so his next choice was to be an air crewman gunner. At 6' 1 1/2" tall, he was simply too tall to fit into any airborne gun turret. Odell was a cheeky kid and couldn't stand the thought that the war might be over and he would not have been a part of it. He returned to the assignment office for another physical. He quickly recorded his height as 5'10" on the official form, and forged a flight surgeon's signature. The forgery went unnoticed and Dobson passed.

After gunnery school in Texas, Odell was assigned to a combat air crew and sent to Wendling, England, where he became a member of the 392nd Bomb Group. By then, the four-engine B-24s had been improved for use in combat by removing the ball turrets, and he was assigned to a waist gunner position, which allowed slightly more room for his height.

Arriving at the assigned barracks, he threw his gear down on his new bunk. A Cajun informed him that he was the third man to occupy that particular bunk in the previous three months. The others were dead.

After twelve successful bombing missions, Staff Sergeant Odell Dobson and his crew were assigned to a B-24 named "Ford's Folly." It happened to be the second B-24 built by Ford Motor Company in Michigan; the first never left the factory. A picture of an elderly black man driving a Model-T was painted on the nose. The plane had been through 79 missions and damaged extensively, then repaired and returned to the group for further missions. It was not a comforting thought.

By this time, it had been over two years since Odell joined the service.

It was September 10, 1944, and pilot C.A. Rudd had been told that if he could fly the plane on 21 more missions, the crew and Ford's Folly would be sent back to the U.S. on a war bond drive. Other crew members that day were Second Lt. J.R. Dawson, navigator; Second Lt. R.J. Benson, co-pilot; Second Lt. W.A. Spencer, bombardier; Tech Sergeant C.R. Maynard, upper turret gunner; Tech Sergeant C.E. Roger Clapp, first radio operator; Staff Sergeant H. Hoganson, right waist gunner; Staff Sergeant R.E. Modlin, nose turret gunner; and Staff Sergeant R.K. Place, tail gunner. The official photograph of the smiling, pleasant-looking crew reveals Dobson standing in the back, conspicuously taller than the rest of his crew.

The members of Combat Crew 3441 were briefed between 4 and 5 a.m. on the morning of September 11. Twenty-four crews received an assignment to attack an ordnance manufacturing depot near Hanover, Germany. It would be a long flight, and as all very well remembered, it was their 13th combat mission.

As they prepared to board Ford's Folly, Tech Sergeant C.R. Maynard noted superstitiously that they should refer to the mission as 12B. Though most admitted to no such superstitions, the question and any foreboding they had was concluded when Tech Sergeant Roger Clapp stated flatly that it was number 13 and they wouldn't be returning.

At 7:30 a.m., the ground rumbled as twenty-four planes fired their engines. The crewmen adjusted uniforms and equipment, and then, in single file, the Liberators taxied to the end of the long runway. Captain Rudd's voice over the intercom announced, "Prepare for takeoff." The great engines roared as the planes lifted off the ground.

Shortly before noon, the group was hit with a flak barrage near the Rhine River. The sky darkened as twenty to thirty German ME 109s circled them, literally blocking out the sun as they attacked. Huge black puffs of smoke filled with flying shards of sharp steel appeared here and there and on all sides. Flak from the explosions tore through the thin B-24 fuselages and all in its path inside.

The canopy on the upper turret was shot away on the first pass, and gunner C.R. Maynard was hit in the head. Within the next few minutes, the nose turret, upper turret, and tail turrets were all disabled. Only the two waist guns now remained functional; it was up to Dobson and Hoganson to battle the attacking enemy planes. Odell fired the 50 caliber waist gun as an ME 109 sidled up against them. He could see the pilot in the enemy plane and aimed directly at him, and squeezed and held down the trigger, just as that pilot broke away under them.

The next fighter was right behind, and his cannon shells hit Odell's gun. The gun exploded, sending hot jagged steel into his legs, side, and face. His goggles snapped in two at the nose piece, and he looked down to see blood dripping profusely into the now dangling single lens. Hoganson, the right waist gunner was also hit and fell on top of Odell. Hoganson got up, holding one hand over his shoulder and resumed his position at his machine gun. He was hit a second time, and got up again. A 20 mm shell tore through his hip, but this time he did not get up. Despite his injuries, Hoganson had managed to stay at his 50 caliber long enough to send three Nazis planes down to earth.

Flying at an altitude of about 27,000 feet, the pilot said, "Hang on boys, I'm going to hit the deck." The mortally wounded plane then went up into a steep climb, stalled out, rolled over to the left, and then spun into a death spiral.

Odell opened the camera hatch. Before bailing out, he took a final look at Staff Sargeant Hoganson, who was slumped over. His eyes were glazed over. Hoganson weakly raised his right hand, then it dropped, lifeless by his side. He then looked at Staff Sargeant R.K. Place, the tail gunner. Place was sitting outside the turret leaning against the bulkhead. His oxygen mask swung to and fro, and blood was running down his face. Odell rolled out of the burning plane as it spun wildly out of control. He tumbled out and lost consciousness.

The official record contained the following eyewitness account of the firefight and demise of Ford's Folly: "Fire in number 3 engine, burst into flames, keeled over, spun in and crashed, no chutes seen..."

The villagers watched as Staff Sergeant Odell Dobson stumbled and fell several times before he realized he wasn't going anywhere. The old man left his plow, and took a sharp stake from his wagon. Odell knew what the villagers were capable of doing, he had heard stories about downed fliers that were beaten to death or burned alive. As the German drew near, Odell pulled out his .45, cocked it, and pointed it at the farmer. The man quickly backed away. Odell slipped the pistol in the front of his jacket. He recalled the only German word he had learned and called out repeatedly, "Komrad!" The man cautiously approached him again, coming up on Odell's blinded left eye, and grabbed his pistol. The angry villagers began shoving him, shouting at him and each other. While they argued, Odell put a tourniquet around one leg. He removed his scarf and fastened it around his other leg. A blonde girl stepped out of the crowd and gently helped him bandage his head.

Prisoner Odell Dobson was helped into the back of a wagon by the blonde girl and an albino boy. He, along with his parachute, were taken to a school building until the villagers could decide what to do with him. He was left alone with the girl, and he watched her rub the fabric of his soft silk parachute between her fingers. Thinking she may have wanted the material for a new dress, he made a motion with his fingers that resembled the cutting movement of scissors. American parachutes were much superior to the broadcloth version that Germans used, and it was essential for him to destroy it to keep the Germans from using it for their own fliers. As the girl went to work hastily cutting up the parachute, a German came in and angrily slapped her hard enough to knock her across the room.

Dobson was taken to the train station where he was amazed to find that Roger Clapp, one of his crew members, was also alive. Roger had parachuted out and landed unharmed, but had been beaten severely by the townspeople. Roger was now a much humbler man than the one Odell had gotten to know. He fancied himself to be some sort of cowboy, and wore his .45 on a low-slung pistol belt that was tied to his leg. He had a switchblade knife that he liked to show off to the other fliers, bragging that before the war was over, his switchblade would have German blood on it. The Roger Clapp that stood before him now was utterly subdued; the earlier Roger gone by reason of war.

The two survivors of Ford's Folly had parachuted near the town of Treis. They were taken to the train station as prisoners of war. Sitting on the ramp at the train station, Odell lit up a cigarette. A German knocked it out of his hand and slapped him in the face. Odell defiantly reached over to pick the cigarette up and the guard stomped it flat. Roger Clapp pleaded with Odell not to make more trouble for them. They were loaded onto a train bound for Giessen.

At Giessen, Odell was taken to a hospital and strapped to a table. Without anesthesia, a surgeon roughly removed the shell fragments from his four wounds. While he recuperated over the next few weeks, he was befriended by a German named Emil Muhl. Emil explained to Odell that the reason for his care and concern was that his mother-in-law was walking his baby son in a stroller one day when an American pilot strafed the town. When he saw the woman and baby, he ceased his strafing run, rolled over slightly, and waved at them before flying off. Emil had a soft spot for American flyers from then on. He offered to help Odell escape, but after extensive planning, it was deemed too risky.

Odell was then moved to a prison hospital in Meinigen. When he had sufficiently recovered, he was sent by train to Kiefheide, a prisoner-of-war camp in northwest Poland.

Stalag Luft IV was a large compound carved out of a forest. It contained about 10,000 prisoners; 2,000 were British, the rest were Americans. Upon his arrival, his warm flight jacket was confiscated to be sent to a German soldier fighting at the Russian front. When the Nazis took his Zippo lighter, Odell demanded a written receipt for his personal effects. A seven-foot guard hit him and knocked him over.

Odell was assigned to a barracks. Other prisoners came streaming in, asking about the status of other fliers they had known or war information he may have heard. To his great surprise, he looked up to see none other than Roger Clapp, the other survivor from Ford's Folly!

On February 5, 1945, the Russian army was advancing through northwest Poland. Though there was negotiation about turning the prisoners over to the Russians, in the end the Germans evacuated the prisoners. The prisoners began a long march to Stargaard, located approximately 150 kilometers away, where they would be housed in an empty factory building.

Instead, they marched over 1200 kilometers over 87 long, cold, and miserable days. The direction of their march changed constantly, as they were kept ahead of the advancing Russian Army.

It was near the end of the war, and food was exceedingly scarce, even for the German military. The prisoners were given three small boiled potatoes at night and an occasional loaf of bread that was divided between three prisoners.

As the forced march progressed, some of the prisoners were too weak and exhausted to continue. Those too ill to travel sat by the side of the road, and after the others passed them by, those who continued to march would hear the sickening sound of gunfire behind them. Thereafter, and in order that they not give up, their comrades helped along the sickest of the stumbling prisoners. Two at a time and until they too were exhausted, they took turns helping the weakest of the men. When they came to a sizable town, the prisoners would sit their sick friends down in the street, hoping someone would take pity on them and get medical help.

When they could find one, they slept in a barn at night. The scrappy prisoners never missed an opportunity to sabotage whatever farm equipment they encountered along the way. They smiled to themselves at the thought of a German farmer losing the wheel of his tractor the next day, or missing some vital gear or implement needed to work the fields. On two occasions, Odell made unsuccessful attempts at escape.

After 56 days of marching, the prisoners were loaded onto "40 et 8" boxcars. Although designed to hold 40 men and 8 of either mules or horses, the men were forced into the cars so tightly that they remained tortuously standing for the entire three day trip. Half were sent south, and Odell was among the half that were sent west. They were greatly relieved when the allied fighters they heard overhead did not mistakenly target the train.

The men finally arrived in Hanover, a prison camp primarily for French prisoners. Among the prisoners were many badly wounded British and American soldiers who had survived the Battle of the Bulge.

After one week, they were again marched out by their German guards. It was during this forced march, and as they approached the Elbe River, that they learned by word-of-mouth that President Roosevelt had died. Odell could not remember who the vice-president was. It was by barge that they crossed the mighty Elbe, as the bridges had been destroyed.

Still they marched. After several days of rest at a German farm, they were ordered to get up and prepare to march. Odell lay down on the floor of the barn with six cigarettes and four matches. He refused to get up. After all he had endured, having been shot down, severely wounded, held prisoner, and nearly starved to death, he declared that he would not take another step, no matter the consequences.

Suddenly, people were running and shouting all around him. It was May 2, 1945. Nazi Germany had surrendered and the prisoners were finally free. Stepping outside to find the source of the commotion, Odell saw a stiff British lieutenant standing up in his jeep. Looking terribly official, he wore a beret, necktie, battle jacket, and of course his revolver. With just he and his driver to deliver the message, he announced, "Gentlemen, you are officially liberated. Disarm your guards and proceed to the town of Buchen."

Considering there was but this one Allied lieutenant and his driver at hand, no one wanted to be the first to grab for a German rifle and begin a firefight with armed guards.

One guard held out his carbine to several prisoners, but they all backed cautiously away. Finally, someone snatched the guard's rifle, whereupon the other prisoners soon disarmed the remainder of the guards.

Odell walked away from captivity with his only surviving crewmate, Roger Clapp. The feeling of intense relief and victory seemed so hollow for Odell; he and Roger were the only survivors of that crew of ten brave American men.

The prisoners made their way into Buchen riding bicycles, wagons, carts, while others walked. They ate real cheese and drank fresh milk at farmhouses along the way. They walked past the bodies of some of their German guards, the more brutal ones that had made life so miserable for the captives. Odell thought the large man that beat him when he asked for a receipt for his belongings was among those who had been shot. He couldn't tell for sure though; the guard's face was gone.

Even after three weeks of freedom, Odell Dobson weighed a scrawny 112 pounds. Not wanting to go home in such an emaciated state, he and other ex-POWs traveled around war-battered Europe, for awhile in a confiscated German officer's luxury Mercedes. It was unbelievably easy to get by in post-war Europe. As an ex-POW, embassies and government agencies of every country eagerly handed over money to help the veterans.

Odell and his friends drove to Camp Lucky Strike near LeHavre, France. German prisoners were put to work dishing out food in the long chow lines, and were instructed by flight surgeons to limit portions for the prisoners so they would not get sick. One ex-POW looked down at the tiny portion of meat he had been served. "Mehr" he said several times. "Nein" was the German's reply. The veteran very deliberately pulled out his P38, jacked a shell into the chamber, and held it to the Nazi's stomach. The German quickly recognized the error of his ways and eagerly shoveled food high onto the American's plate.

Odell was officially AWOL for more than two months before he finally boarded an LST (Landing Ship, Tank) in Plymouth, England and sailed for 17 1/2 days to Newport News, Virginia. Thus it was that in July 1945, Sgt. Dobson again walked on American soil.

Over the years, Odell has recounted his story many times. His recalls details of incidents as if they had just happened. As with those memories, his battle scars will always remain. His regrets run the gamut: that he didn't have the opportunity to fly a greater number of missions, that all of his crewmates did not survive, and that he took a hat from a German officer when he pleaded with Odell to let him keep it as his own.

The crewmen killed on the mission were interred outside the consecrated ground of a village cemetery in Germany.   They were eventually reinterred - one in Newport, Indiana, three in St. Louis, Missouri, and four in Margraten, Holland.

Years later, Odell contacted his crewmate Roger Clapp, then a resident of California. Fifteen minutes into their first phone conversation, Roger chastised him for stubbornly trying to smoke a cigarette after the German guard slapped him.   Roger's demons never left him, it seemed.   When Odell made plans to fly to California to see him, Roger called him the night before and informed him that he would not be there. Roger died without seeing Odell again.

Odell and his wife Barbara have lived in Decatur, Alabama since 1961. They have three grown children, two sons and a daughter. A twinkle still comes to Odell's eye when he recounts the pranks they pulled on their Nazi captors. He holds no grudges and he harbors no bitterness. He quit smoking in 1988.

On September 11, 1944, four American bombers of the 392nd Bomb Group were shot down over Germany. Ford's

Folly was among those casualties. Six German ME 109s were also shot down. The mission was officially declared a success for the Allied Forces.

The Tragedy of Tom Dooley

"Hang Down Your Head Tom Dooley, Hang Down Your Head and Cry…"

The words to this song are familiar to Americans of a certain age as the hit song the Kingston Trio made famous in the late 1950s. What most Americans do not know is that this ballad was first penned some 130 years ago by unknown mountain folk of North Carolina. Based on a true story and a man named Tom Dula, this story is about a man who some believed was executed for a crime he did not commit.

In the late Spring of 1865, Southerners welcomed home their tired and starving men who fought for the Confederacy. Wilkes County, North Carolina residents opened their arms to the lifeblood of their community too. Among them was a handsome twenty-one-year-old man named Tom Dula.

Dula joined the Confederacy in 1862 at the age of 17. He was a private in Co. K, 42nd Regiment, North Carolina

Infantry. Dula had been captured by the Union Army, and was in the Federal prison known as Point Lookout in Maryland, when General Robert E. Lee surrendered. Like other released prisoners, Dula was required to sign an oath of allegiance to the U.S. Government before his freedom was granted. He signed it two different ways - Dula, his given name, and Dooley, the name recorded by the Union guard unaccustomed to words pronounced with the Southern dialect. Tom had two older brothers who also fought for the South, but he was the only one to survive.

Tom Dula began his long walk back to the hills of North Carolina with only one certainty in his future, a life of extreme poverty.

"Hang down your head Tom Dooley, poor boy you're bound to die!"

Dula appeared to live a life unencumbered by moral boundaries. He lived with his widowed mother, but spent much time with a beautiful married woman named Ann Foster Melton. Although Ann had married in her early teens, she carried on an illicit relationship with Dula, to the apparent indifference of her husband. Also involved with Dula was Ann's cousin, Pauline Foster. Pauline moved into James and Ann Melton's home to be near a doctor who was treating her for the pock, a mountain term for venereal disease.

There was yet another cousin of Pauline and Ann whose fate was intertwined with theirs. She was an attractive girl named Laura Foster, who stole her father's mare early one Friday morning to run off and marry her lover, Tom Dula.

"I met her on the mountain, there I took her life. Met her on the mountain, stabbed her with my knife."

What happened that day can only be pieced together by circumstantial evidence brought out in court records.

On Friday, May 25, 1866, Tom Dula made an early morning visit to Laura's home where he awakened her before daybreak. After they spoke softly, he left on foot, and Laura quietly dressed and packed a few belongings. She left shortly after, without waking her widowed father or four younger siblings. Riding astride her father's mare, she met a woman on the road and explained that she was going to meet Tom so they could go away to get married. Besides Laura's killer, the woman on the road was the last person to see her alive.

Laura's disappearance initially invoked her father's anger for stealing his horse. When the horse returned the next day with a broken tether, the community began to grow alarmed.

Rumors, speculation, and concerns about Laura's fate settled across the mountain ridge like a cold winter fog. Tom Dula was stoically silent. Men came from miles around to establish a search party for Laura's body. The broken missing half of the horse's tether was found tied to a tree on the mountain ridge near a dark spot on the ground that was thought to be human blood.

All eyes turned to Tom, who remained unworried about Laura's disappearance. The townspeople found it peculiar that he did not volunteer to join the search party, a strange reaction for a man whose bride-to-be simply vanished.

One month after Laura's disappearance, Tom had his worn boots repaired and walked out of Happy Valley, determined to disappear in Tennessee.

"This time tomorrow, reckon where I'll be, Hadn't it been for Grayson, I'd be in Tennessee."

By the time Tom's boots wore out again, he was at the farm of Col. James Grayson, a former Union officer, prominent farmer, and legislator. Tom changed his name and worked on Grayson's farm long enough to earn the money for a new pair of boots. Once again he began his journey away from his past.

Shortly after Tom's departure, sheriff's deputies arrived at Col. Grayson's farm to arrest Tom for the assumed murder of Laura Foster. Tom's sudden move, and his attempt to hide his identity, made him the prime suspect.

Charges were brought against Tom Dula and his lover Ann Foster Melton. Although Laura was still missing, authorities felt that there was enough evidence based on an incident related by Pauline Foster. She claimed that Ann Melton frantically tried to show her Laura's grave in a moment of panic and guilt.

Tom and Ann were held in adjoining cells in the Wilkesboro jail when on September 1, 1866, Laura's decomposed body was found in a shallow grave, ironically by a distant cousin of Tom's. Laura's legs were drawn up to fit into the hole which was too small for her body. Her decomposed face looked upward. A six-inch gaping stab wound to her chest was the apparent cause of her death.

The prosecution's case against Tom was pieced together by the testimony of various witnesses who told of a young man angry enough to kill Laura Foster, the woman he blamed for giving him venereal disease. Ann Melton was charged as the person who put him up to the deed. Her motive was jealousy over Laura and Tom's relationship. Although Tom was defended by ex-North Carolina Governor Zebulon Vance, he was found guilty and sentenced to hang. A legal loophole granted him a second trial. The inevitable was prolonged through delays, appeals, and witnesses who failed to show up in court. Once again however, Tom was found guilty and sentenced to hang.

"This time tomorrow, reckon where I'll be, Down in some lonesome valley, hanging from a white oak tree."

Nearly two years after Laura's death, Tom Dula, the handsome young ex-Confederate who had only three months of formal education and an admirable war record, languished in the jail cell, counting down his final moments. Perhaps the carnage of war or some diminished value of human life brought him to the gallows on May 1, 1868. Up until the night before his execution, he claimed his innocence. In the dark hours of April 30, he wrote a declaration stating that he alone was responsible for the death of Laura Foster. Skeptics felt he was trying to free Ann Melton.

On May 1, he rode in a wagon carrying the simple coffin that would bear his body back to Happy Valley, North Carolina. In front of a large crowd of people, he stood as the noose was placed around his neck. He remarked on the clean rope, and made a ghoulish comment that he should have come that day with a clean neck. The wagon was moved from under him and because the fall did not break his neck, he slowly strangled to death, taking the whole truth with him to the grave.

"Hang down your head and cry, poor boy, you're bound to die. Poor boy, you're bound to...die!"

John Foster West, who wrote two books on the subject and is a descendant of people who figured prominently in the case, speculated on the actual events based on his extensive research. Pauline Foster was most likely the person who gave Tom Dula venereal disease, and he in turn passed it on to Ann Melton and Laura Foster. There seems to be little doubt that Ann, Tom, and Laura were together on that day, but which of the two suspects committed the actual murder will never be known.

Ann Melton died some years later, although accounts of her death differ. One suggests she died as a result of advanced syphilis. Another says she died when a wagon turned over on her. In her lifetime, many who knew the trio held Ann responsible for Laura's death.

The site of Laura's murder is now known as Laura Foster Ridge. Tom Dula's headstone, although inscribed with an incorrect date of death, has become an unfortunate target of vandals who have hacked off pieces for souvenirs.

Corporal John Stewart

Corporal John Stewart

John Stewart and his brother Jeff were from a close family. Eight children were born to their parents, Thomas and Birdie Stewart, in the tiny community of Greenbrier, Alabama. John and Jeff worked on their father's cotton farm and helped out in the family country store until they were drafted into the U.S. Army in 1941.

The following story contains excerpts from their wartime letters to their sister Ellen Stewart Hundley. Jeff was in the service briefly and there were only a few letters from him. These letters paint a poignant picture of the loneliness and hardships felt by soldiers everywhere. Ellen, who faithfully wrote them words of encouragement, kept all 61 of their cards and letters neatly tied with a pink ribbon.

The grammar and spelling have been retained as written.

"June 4, 1941, Camp Wheeler, Georgia...I am sorry you felt like you did about me not writing but I won't let it happen again. I might not get to write so often, but I will write as often as I can. You don't have to wait for me to write. You know I can't write as

often as you can. I made it back to Camp OK. I have been feeling blue since I come back. I sure did hate to leave so quick Sun. I don't mind this place but I had rather be a home…Tell all I said hello. Your Brother, John."

Ellen chided the boys for not writing more promptly. They were constantly having to apologize and promise to do better.

"June 13, 1941, Camp Stewart, Georgia…How are you all now? I am O.K. I am coming home the 21th of this month. I sure will be glad. I can't hardly wate. I thought it would be the 26th. I swaped furlough with another boy. He was supposed to get his the 21th. He said he rather have his the 26th that suited me because I wanted to go home as soon as I can. I will get five days. Have you all had any rain yet it rained here Sunday an a little yesterday…We haven't spent the night in the woods in a good while. I am glad of that because I didn't like that sleeping on the ground. I am in the Battery with the boys that has been here since Feb. I am under a different Sargent. I like him lots better than the one I was with at first. We don't drill much now. I like moast of the boys here it seems like I have been knowing them for a long time…Your Brother, Jeff"

When John and Jeff left for the service, they had never been away from home before. They were Alabama plow boys and had not known any other life. They were terribly homesick and hoped to be back at home soon.

"*July 23, 1941, Camp Stewart, Georgia...I got your letter this morning. How are you all by now? I have had a bad cold. It sure is hot here. But we don't have to work much hard. I went to see Buck Private last Sun. night. I mean that sure was a funny picture. How does the crops look now? I guess you all are getting plenty of rain. I went back to the range last Friday to practice shooting my rifle. I did a little beter this time than I did at first, but it really made my arm sore. Well I don't know much to write. I will stop. Write to me soon. Love, Jeff*"

Jeff wrote to his young niece:

"*...I don't like the Army much. Don't many of the boys here like it. I like the boys here in the tent...*"

"*August 10, 1941, Camp Stewart, Georgia...It is really hot here. We had a review Friday. You could look acros the Praide ground an see soldiers falling out some times it would be two or three at the time fall out but the most of them was Yankees didn't but one out of our battery fall out. I made it pretty well of course I got pretty hot. I went to the show Monday night to see Caught in the Draft that was really a good picture. It was kindly like Buck Private...Your Brother, Jeff*"

"*August 23, 1941, Alexandria, Louisiana...Guess you thought I was not going to write but I really haven't had time. I have really been going this week. The 172nd is in reserves but still we have to follow around, and usually it is on foot. We hiked most every day last week and haven't fired a shot yet...It is plenty*" *of snakes here. Lots of rattlers and coil snakes. It has been several found in different tents, and lots of the boys have been bit. Don't tell Mama and Papa about it. They would only worry more...The officers here sure are good. I make it fine with them...I slept one night, what little I did sleep on the ground without a blanket or anything to sleep on. I used my water cup for a pillow. It was also sprinkling rain. I never had all my clothes off all last week. We had to be ready to pull out anytime of the night...Write soon, Love, John"*

Army life was much different than anything they had known before. The Stewart children had always spent Sunday together at their parents' home with plenty of fried chicken, turnip greens, and corn bread. Afterwards, they enjoyed pitching horseshoes and playing checkers with anyone who stopped by.

"September 17, 1941, Camp Stewart, Georgia...We went down on Mond. we had to pitch our tents in grass nearly knee high an the grass was wet. It rained Mon. night in my tent...How is Bill's crops? Have you heard from John lately? I guess I had better stop an go to bed...Love, Jeff"

"September 20, 1941, Eunice, Louisiana...How is everyone feeling? I am feeling fine except some blisters on my feet. They are about well now. I haven't heard a mail call this week and I sure would like to hear one. You said you was going to make some candy and I could hardly wait to get it, and I haven't had a

chance to know if I got it...How does Papa seem to be feeling now. I worry lots about him too. I worry lots about all of you. I sure get homesick at times. It has been almost three months since I have been home. It sure helps lots when I get mail from home. I can't write near as often as I would like to. In the last two months since I have been here I bet I have started over a hundred letters and never get to finish them. I guess people out in Civillian life will make lots of money this fall with cotton a good price and so many jobs are available. I sure wish I was out of here now. The shoe shine boy's and paper boy's are making more than I am. Try and get Papa and Mama to take care of themselves. Write soon, Your Brother, John"

The whole country was pulling out of the deep abyss carved by the Depression. The economy was finally good, but John was furious to hear about the workers on strike for higher wages. Soldiers like him made so little.

"October 1, 1941, Alexandria, Louisiana...I think we leave for Blanding Friday. I sure will be glad to get out of these La. woods...I sure was afraid of snakes when I first came here. It was more rattlers here than I believe there was any place. After a week or two, I soon got used to them...I picked up my blanket the other day and one crawled out of it. I am glad to get away from them. Write often, John"

In the same envelope, John sent a letter to his niece:

"…You sure will be dressed up with all the clothes you said you have. You will have to divide some of them with your kittens this winter. Time you clothe all them you won't have many left. How about swapping you some snakes for part of them? Well I gotta hush now. Write again - John"

Jeff Stewart was anxious to get out of the Army under the newly-passed rule that anyone over age 28 was eligible for a discharge. On October 3, 1941, he wrote his last letter to Ellen before coming back home to Greenbrier:

"…I don't know yet when I am going to get out I thank the paper has been sent to N.C. They will have to be signed up by the Cornel an come back it takes a good while to get any thang like that straight. Was the fair good at Huntsville? How is Bill getting with gathering his cotton? Answer soon. Love, Jeff"

John Stewart went to high school in Tanner. He was movie-star handsome with pearly white teeth. Even a scar on his face he received while chopping wood did not detract from his appearance. He was popular and had a good sense of humor. John was born in 1918, next to the youngest in the family. Of all the Stewart children, John was his father's favorite.

"October 25, 1941, Camp Blanding, Florida…Yes you did wait a long time to write. I began to think you wasn't going to answer. The cookies sure was good. There was several boys in my tent when I got them. I passed them around. You should have

heard them bragging about them. I sure was proud to get them...I can hardly wait until Dec. so that I can come home. Some time I just hate this place then again it is all-right...I know Jeff is proud to be home. I know about how he feels..."

John had been engaged to be married, but the relationship ended before he was drafted. Ellen had apparently asked him if he heard from his former sweetheart. He told her he had received a letter from her, but did not elaborate.

"November 13, 1941, Ft. Jackson, South Carolina...How you like this cold weather? I don't like it so well myself. Especially out here sleeping on the ground. Wake up in the morning's covered with frost...I heard that Roosevelt said he wanted all the soldiers back at their base camp by the 25th. Said that it was so many sick...How does Mama and Papa seem to be feeling now? I am afraid they worry too much about me. I get so blue at times here I don't know what to do. At times I make it fine. I will appreciate cookies or candy any time. While we are on maneuvers we don't get half enough to eat. Some mornings we eat breakfast about three or four and that probably won't be nothing but a egg and then we have one sandwich for dinner then have supper about ten or eleven..."

John's letters constantly expressed his concern that his parents worried about him too much. After the United

States declared war on Japan, John's letters took on a more somber tone. He knew he wouldn't be coming home soon.

"December 13, 1941, Camp Blanding, Florida…I wasn't a bit surprised when war was declared I have been expectin it all time…Don't let it worry you any. I think we will soon get the best of them. You know we have lots more to fight for than they have, so we have got to win…I will finish this letter if that siren ever stop's. We have had practice blackouts…"

He wrote to his young niece:

"…What is Santa going to bring you this year? He has already come to see me and brought me a rifle and ammunition so I guess I will have to try to help him by using it…"

"January 1, 1942, Camp Blanding, Florida…I never did tell you how much I appreciated the Xmas present but you know I did without telling you. I just know Papa will be sick now. I have never seen him take on so like he did when I left. He is afraid I will have to go across…"

To his niece, John wrote:

"…I don't know where we are going yet. Mabie where the kangroos live or mabie where savages live or no telling where…"

At this point, John's letters all bore the mark of a censor. He told Ellen that he wouldn't be able to tell the family where he was going or what he was doing, and that Ellen's husband Bill, who had served in World War I, could explain to her why. His mail went to an APO San Francisco address.

"May 10, 1942…The one (letter) I got this morning was the one that you had the 91st Psalm written. I had just sat down for breakfast when I got it. I read it before I eat. This was a good time to receive it. It being Sunday morning. I have never paid any attention to that chapter but it is a good one. Today is Mother's Day. Although I have been up for the last few nights I am going to try to go to Church this morning. I sure do appreciate you writing to me as often as you do. I think I got more mail from you than any of them…I am alway's thinking of all you…"

"…Thou shalt not be afraid for the terror by night; nor for the arrow that flieth by day;…For He shall give His angels charge over thee, to keep thee in all thy ways. They shall bear thee up in their hands, lest thou dash thy foot against a stone…" *Psalm 91: 5, 11, 12.*

"June 28, 1942…I guess when they start rationing gas you will have to go down home on the train, won't you? How is crops this year? Good? They should bring a good price this fall, better than last fall…"

"July 9, 1942…I would like to see you all now. I would never get over being homesick. I am always thinking of you. Ellen keep writing often and tell me all the new's…"

John was close to his nieces and nephews who were nearer in age to him than his older brothers and sisters. Once he was out in the field at Greenbrier with his brothers and an assortment of nieces and nephews, looking down into a sink hole. They decided collaboratively, that someone must have buried gold in the hole, maybe even during the Civil War. John was sent home to get a pick-ax and while he was gone, the others hastily buried an empty five gallon can. It was getting dark, but John commenced to digging and when he struck the can, he was so excited. Of course, he laughed too when he discovered the truth.

"July 19, 1942…Can you imagine. I also saw the picture of James Stewart in training in the Air Corp's. Just a little over a month from the time you saw it, until the time it was shown here. They have some new films now so the show's are not so very old…The theater is built out in the open, just hard plank seat's but we could not expect any better there. We are lucky to even have that. It help's lot's to see a picture now and then. That is the only kind of amusement we do have…I have about got use to the rat's and lizzard's crawling around on me. They use to keep me awake…"

"August 2, 1942…I guess cotton has began to open there now? I guess it's plenty hot too?…We are due for a rest, although we may not get it. We need to get where we can get some good food such as milk, eggs, and fresh fruit and meat's.

About all we got here is hash and bean's. We have to eat that stuff much longer we won't be able to do anything. I have lost plenty of weight since I left the states..."

"August 9, 1942...We caught a large turtle last night. It weighed around three hundred pounds. It was about three feet wide and about four feet long. I took a picture of it..."

"August 17, 1942...Wonder how come Louis to quit school? Some day he will be sorry...Yes Ellen I get enough sweet's, such as they are..."

One day, John's sister Estelle received a letter from him with a strange statement that seemed inappropriate. She ran down to her father's store waving the letter in her hand to show them, so they could help figure out his code. He wrote, *"Can Aunt Nell Take Over Now?"* By taking the first letter of every word, they realized that he was referring to Canton Island, an uninhabited atoll in the central Pacific Ocean. Canton is situated about 1,800 miles southwest of Honolulu, and is part of the Phoenix island chain. A weather station was established on Canton in 1938 by the United States.

"September 20, 1942...I am in the Hawaiian Island's now. I don't know how the mail service is going to be here..."

"November 15, 1942...Well another Sunday. I can hardly keep up with the day's here. One day is the same as the other anyhow. If Roy likes to quarrel and fight so well they should put

him in the Army. Everyone in Civillian life is making good money. If they are not it's their fault. No there are no beautiful girl's here like everyone think's there is…I sure wish I could be home Xmas. It will be my first Xmas to ever spend away from home. But I am not the only one. There are thousand's more that this will be their first…"

The first picture John had made in his uniform showed a smiling, happy young man. Sometime after his promotion, he had another picture made. The smiling young man from the first picture now looked terribly haggard and tired.

"November 28, 1942…I received a letter and the Xmas present's this week that you sent me. Everything was so nice that you sent. The cigarette's came in at the right time. I was out and had just borrowed a pack. I was proud of the book's you sent especially the Readers Digest. I haven't been able to find one over here. I like to read them, they are alway's very interesting. I don't remember the letter that I wrote you thought so much of. Well I am still making it fine. Just hoping that war will soon be over and I can come home again. I have often thought of the times when Mama told me I did not know how to appreciate a good home. If I ever get back I will. Life is just what you make it. You can make it miserable or you can make it satisfactory any place. Some times you may feel awful blue but only yourself can get you out of that. I know I am here and I try to make the best of it I can.

Sometimes it is hard to look and feel cheerful but I alway's think there is someone in lot's worse places and having a lot's harder time than I am, so I feel that I have lot's to be thankful for. I hope to see victory and see it soon and hope that no one can ever say John failed to do his part..."

John sent money to his older sister Ola, to buy each of his brothers and sisters a Bible as his Christmas present to them.

"December 14, 1942...I will write you a few lines to let you know I am alright. I know you were disappointed not hearing from me one week, but I just didn't have the time to write...Billy Don (Ellen's son) wanted to know if there was any Cocoanut's here. Tell him I was eating one when I got your letter..."

"January 8, 1943...No I did not know the boy that got killed that you ask me about. You said that Bob wrote home quite often, where is he anyhow? Do they hear from Joe very often? I guess they do though...So you think you will visit this place (Hawaii) after the war is over? I guess after the war is over I will never be satisfied in one place long, but the way I feel now when I get home I will stay there..."

John once gave his young nephew a pipe to smoke when he finally got tired of his pestering. His nephew was sick for the rest of the day and, out of guilt, John had to pull him everywhere in the back of a wagon.

"*April 24, 1943...Mama said you always ask about me the first thing when you went down home and alway's told them if you had heard from me. I just got through writing a letter to her...*"

"*June 24, 1943...Glad you liked the shell's. Mama was proud of her's...*"

John wrote as often as he could to all of his brothers and sisters, nieces and nephews. He said to Ellen once that he didn't understand why his brother Bill had never once written a letter to him.

"*August 16, 1943...This is the first letter to you since I arrived in Australia so by the time you get this you will already know I am here. I like here fine and am feeling good. I like the people alright. I like to hear some of the talk. A few nights ago I was talking to a Scotchman. Everyone was laughing at him talk, but he didn't mind. He had seen a good bit of action and he had the scars to show for it...*"

"*September 19, 1943...There is some funny looking animals here. Some one caught a large lizard the other day, or that is what we called it. It was about four feet long and had a forked tongue that was about six inches long...*"

"*November 6, 1943 Dear Ellen,*

I received a letter from you to-day. Was glad to hear from you. I am getting along OK. Thank's for the picture you sent...I haven't much time to do any writing I have to wash some clothes today. Some of the boy's have a pet possum here and the thing has just crawled in my pocket and went to sleep.

I will write again when I have time. Love Bro. Jno."

This was John's final letter to his sister Ellen. Included in the package of letters Ellen saved, were yellowed newspaper clippings published in December, 1943.

"Limestone Boy Reported Dead in Foreign Zone.

Mr. and Mrs. T.J. Stewart of Greenbrier were notified by wire early this week that their fine young son, John Stewart, had died while in the service of his country. The young man, it is presumed, was killed in action, although this was not definitely stated in the wire.

We understand that the parents received two letters yesterday morning from their son..."

Corporal John Wesley Stewart died on December 2, 1943 as a result of wounds he received November 30. He was 26 years old. Years later, John was brought back home. After a memorial service in Greebrier, he was buried in Madison, Alabama.

Ellen also saved a Christmas card that she had bought and signed, but never sent, to her beloved brother John.

John Stewart in Australia - WWII

The Price of Justice

The 1930s marked a dark period in the history of Alabama. This is a story about one Alabama man who stood tall in his decision to uphold justice and change the course of history, a decision that cost him his political career.

In March, 1931, Victoria Price and Ruby Bates hopped a freight train in Chattanooga bound for Huntsville, Alabama. In those Depression days, Ruby and Victoria were known to be some-time prostitutes and had the jail records to prove it. Among the other illegal passengers on the train were nine black men aged 13 to 20. When the train stopped in Scottsboro, about 15 deputized men met the train to check out the claim of a disturbance reported by white men who had been thrown off of the train near Stevenson. Everyone was told to leave the train, and the two women at first tried to run away. Twenty minutes later, they claimed to the deputies that they had been raped by "the nine black boys."

Judge Alred Hawkins of Scottsboro presided as a grand jury voted to indict the men. The judge appointed all seven of Scottsboro's attorneys to represent the men, but six reported conflicts. One attorney claimed that he represented the Alabama Power Company, who stood to profit financially if the accused were electrocuted. In a frenzy of moral outrage, all of the young men were tried, convicted, and sentenced to die by electrocution within a few weeks of the event. However, the U.S. Supreme Court overturned the convictions based on inferior defense counsel, and the judge granted the request for a change of venue.

In March 1933, the trial of the "Scottsboro Boys" landed squarely in the lap of Judge James Edward Horton, Jr., circuit court judge in Morgan County, Alabama.

Judge Horton was assigned to the case of the Scottsboro Boys by the Chief Justice of the Supreme Court. The 6'4" judge was soft-spoken, tolerant, witty, and a good story-teller. He had received a classical education at Cumberland University, with five years of Latin and four years of Greek. He was a member of the Presbyterian Church in Athens, Alabama, and attended regularly until gas rationing came into effect during World War II. By then the family had moved to the country, and although he no longer attended the church some 15 miles away, he continued to contribute financially.

From the beginning, Judge Horton's trial would be different. He had reserved spaces in the courtroom for out-of-town newspaper reporters. The townspeople already resented the interference of northerners sent down to criticize Alabama's justice system. The judge even incensed the onlookers when he shook the hand of a black reporter.

According to Judge Horton, one of the doctors who examined the two women told him confidentially in the men's restroom, that there was no way the women could have been raped. He refused to testify to the truth, however, because he was afraid he would lose his practice, and he had only been out of medical school for three years. The judge considered declaring a mistrial, but changed his mind because he felt sure that twelve intelligent men would recognize that the story fabricated by the two prostitutes, were full of lies. Unfortunately, some people at that time actually believed that if a white woman was alone with a black man, he would not be able to resist molesting her.

The prosecution's case appeared to be in trouble when one of the female accusers reversed her story and admitted that the women had made the whole thing up. Samuel Liebowitz, a New York attorney hired by the International

Labor Defense and reluctantly backed by the NAACP, argued for the defense. Ruby Bates, the woman who recanted her story, appeared in fine clothing after spending time in the northeast speaking at rallies to free the Scottsboro Boys. But her appearance and new-found celebrity status only proved, in the eyes of the townspeople, that "those people from up north" had bought her off.

Ironically, women and black men were not allowed to serve on the jury because they were considered too unintelligent to understand complex legal terminology.

Unfortunately for the defendants, Judge Horton had miscalculated the jury, and they immediately came back with a verdict of guilty. Punishment was set at death.

After carefully writing more than 26 pages of brief to support his decision, Judge Horton set aside the verdict and ordered another trial. The backlash against the judge was immediate. He was applauded outside his state, but only one newspaper, which happened to be in Birmingham, backed his decision. The voters in his home state made their wrath known in the next election. Judge Horton must have anticipated the public anger over his decision. He had already been warned that his interference in swift justice would sound the death knell on his political career.

The retrials continued under Judge William Callahan, who presided in the manner the people demanded. Many locals waited for news of the trials near the statue of Lady Justice, outside the Morgan County Courthouse. Judge Callahan did not bother to hide his contempt for the defense attorney of the nine on trial, and refused to allow important testimony, including that of Ruby Bates. Not surprisingly, they were again found guilty.

Although Horton carried the counties of Limestone and Lawrence in the 1934 election, he was still defeated and never served on the bench again. It was understood that he lost the election over the trial of the Scottsboro Boys, but he never once doubted his decision or had any regrets. He believed that justice was the right of everyone, no matter what color or sex, and he could not have lived with himself if he had not fought for their rights as he did. His personal philosophy was "fiat justitia ruat coelum," or "let justice be done though the heavens may fall."

The Scottsboro Boys endured many painful years in prison, until they were eventually released under the relentless pressure of various organizations and people convinced of their innocence. The trials had brought the attention of the President of the United States, as well as people all over the world.

Judge Horton died at the age of 95 and is buried in Athens, Alabama.

Many have wondered why these women made the claim that ruined so many innocent people. It has been surmised that they were in violation of the Mann Act on that March day in 1931, and by making the accusations, they were in effect, drawing attention elsewhere. Victoria Price's crime was that she had illegally crossed the state line with a man other than her husband.

Over 70 years have passed since the infamous trials of the Scottsboro Boys. Alabama has come a long way from the dark days of oppression, although the reputation lingers ever close. It is appropriate that we recognize the integrity of Judge Ed Horton and the proud legacy he left to our state, as well as his family. Based on his courage and legal ability, Judge James Edward Horton is considered one of the top ten State trial judges in American history.

Old Georgia Graveyard

Some suggested it was under the parking lot. Those who remember still get angry about it. Others speculated that it was some ancient Indian burial ground. The truth is that Huntsville Hospital is built over a cemetery, where burials were still taking place in the early 1900s.

1819 brought statehood to Alabama, but Huntsville was already a thriving community by then. Alabama's first Constitutional Convention was held in Walker Allen's cabinet shop, the largest vacant building in the city. Prominent citizens whose names became synonymous with forging the fledgling city, were acquiring vast amounts of property and building mansions that have withstood nearly 200 years of war, weather, and urban renewal.

One of the many transactions, as recorded in Deed Book G, page 183 in the Madison County Courthouse, shows that on September 3, 1818, LeRoy Pope and his wife Judith sold property to the city of Huntsville for $75. The surveyor's report describes it as being on the west side of the Meridian Road leading to Ditto's Landing and on David Moore's north boundary. Described as "two acres more or less," it was sold for the express purpose of a graveyard for the town of Huntsville.

It is the popular belief that the 1818 land sale was the beginning of present-day Maple Hill Cemetery, however, it was actually the burial ground that came to be known as "Georgia." Although the specific reason for that name is unknown, it has been suggested that it was because many of the area's first settlers moved to Huntsville from Petersburg, Georgia. Georgia Cemetery was originally established as a white city cemetery, but even early on, slaves were buried there as well.

After only four years, Georgia Cemetery was deemed unsuitable for burial of white people due to the flooding that kept it a swamp most of the time. After only four years, LeRoy Pope sold the city another tract of land that would later come to be known as Maple Hill Cemetery.

While the local white population used Maple Hill for burials, Georgia continued to be used as a cemetery for black interments only. By 1870, the black cemetery known as Glenwood was founded, and it is assumed that only occasional burials were held at Georgia Cemetery, probably because it was nearly full. Two acres of land would hold at least 2,000 bodies. Huntsville's 1870 population was 7-

9,000, and approximately 40% of the residents were black. In 1861, there were 1,591 slaves living in Huntsville proper. Even though many black people would have been buried on plantations, it is still possible that Georgia Cemetery was nearly full by 1870. Construction work at the Georgia site in recent years has unearthed graves that can be traced to the early part of this century by clothing and casket styles that clearly indicate Georgia Cemetery was used for burials in this century.

In 1820, Georgia Cemetery became the important focal point of the historic Huntsville African Baptist Church. Slaves first met under dogwood trees planted as temporary shelter for members gathered to hear God's word delivered by their first pastor, William Harris. In 1833, a law was enacted that forbid slaves to gather unless there was a white man present who could prevent slaves from discussing or planning freedom. Sermons were even censored for the same reason. A church building was erected, and years later during the Civil War, Reverend Bartley Harris was secretly known as someone to trust with the safekeeping of valuables sought after by Union soldiers.

Bartley Harris must have felt a dilemma in his own mind. He risked his own life by saving their valuables during the war. He could easily have somehow sold those valuables to buy his freedom or finance his escape north, but Bartley Harris was first and foremost, a Christian man.

Misfortune's heavy hand dealt a blow to the church when it was burned by Union soldiers who occupied Huntsville during the Civil War. After the war, President Ulysses Grant appropriated money for rebuilding the church, which was rededicated in 1872 in a nearby location, and named St. Bartley in respect for the saintly behavior of their beloved pastor, who baptized some 3,000 people in his lifetime.

Madison County Deed Book 92, page 275 contains the description of land known as "Longwood Plantation" that came into the sole ownership of Harry M. Rhett on November 7, 1903. The surveyor's report in the deed referred to the south boundary of the African Cemetery. The cemetery is also pictured in the original 1903 Quigley map of Huntsville. The fragile book which contains this map clearly shows the Georgia Cemetery identified simply as "Colored Cemetery."

The demise and destruction of the Georgia Cemetery started in the early 1900s. Local legend says that a black man assaulted a white person and caused anger and outrage in the white community. An incensed mob of white people took their vengeance on the black community by knocking down headstones and causing destruction in the cemetery and the surrounding fence. Another version suggests that the vandalism to Georgia Cemetery was a gradual process.

On June 30, 1925, Harry and Louise Rhett deeded a tract of land to the city for the construction of Huntsville Hospital. In an act of benevolence and charity on the part of the Rhetts, it was specifically stated that the Colored Cemetery that bordered this tract of land must be maintained by the city and conditions were spelled out in the event the city failed to keep up its side of the bargain.

Less than three weeks later on July 19, 1925, the city of Huntsville gave the recently-acquired Rhett property to the corporation identified as The Huntsville Hospital. For reasons unknown, the surveyor's description did not contain any mention of the cemetery that bordered it, and even contained the sentence, "…it is seized in fee thereof and that the same are free from encumbrances."

The hospital was erected adjacent to the Georgia Cemetery, and for some period of time, the cemetery was largely ignored. Remaining headstones gradually disappeared or were moved off, and Georgia Cemetery appeared to be another vacant lot. By the 1940s, people began parking their cars over it, and urban sprawl began to force black people in the surrounding neighborhood out. The swampy character was corrected in the 1950s when a drainage system was installed. Those who remembered it as a cemetery were moved out and uninformed, or perhaps deliberate rumors circulated that it was an ancient Indian burial ground.

Huntsville's dynamic growth of the 1960s necessitated an expanded hospital system. On September 28, 1961, the City of Huntsville presented another deed to the Hospital Building Authority. The deed contained the property originally deeded by Harry Rhett, which describes it as being along the south margin of the Colored Cemetery. To confuse matters further, in the same document the city also deeded the property originally sold by LeRoy Pope and his wife Judith in 1818. In that description however, there was absolutely no mention of any cemetery, even though it referred to the 1818 deed. The hospital then built an extension over the cemetery, and for all intents and purposes, it was as if Georgia Cemetery never existed.

The second site of what became known as St. Bartley Primitive Baptist Church, which was rebuilt after the war, became another casualty of Huntsville's growth. Property around the hospital was condemned and that area encompassed St. Bartley Church. St. Bartley moved to the present location on Belafonte. Today, St. Bartley is a thriving, growing, and beautiful church, one that Rev. Bartley Harris would be most proud of. Older members however, still recall the little cemetery named Georgia, with an extreme sense of sorrow.

Finally, what of the people originally interred in Georgia Cemetery? Were they relocated? Perhaps they are yet resting under a memorial of tons of glass and concrete.

Rest in peace, Georgia Cemetery.

Epilogue

This story was originally published under my pen name, Leslie Jeffreys, the first names of my children. Reverend Dr. William Gladys answered the many questions I had regarding the astounding history of St. Bartley Primitive Baptist Church, for use in this story.

On November 3, 2000, a play based on the story of St. Bartley P.B. Church was performed by students of the Academy of Science and Foreign Languages. It premiered before the congregation and guests of St. Bartley Primitive Baptist Church in Huntsville, Alabama. Reverend Dr. William T. Gladys, Pastor of St. Bartley Primitive Baptist Church, and the congregation of this historic church, honored me with a dozen roses and a certificate of recognition.

To the gracious and kind members and pastor of St. Bartley Primitive Baptist Church, I would once again like to say, thank you.

Abandon Ship!

By Leslie Gray and Jacque Gray

"Mac, Mac, is that you?" Harold Oleson shouted through the black smoke, the horrendous noise, and the devastation. His friend Clayton "Mac" McQuay was all but invisible.

"Come get me Harold!" Clayton McQuay desperately shouted back at his friend on the lifeboat. McQuay gasped for air as he struggled to hold on to the slick wing of an upside-down seaplane that had been pitched into the harbor after the explosion. He was covered with pitch black fuel oil, and his friend was able to recognize him only by the sound of his voice. The fire was twenty feet away and getting closer. Oleson worked frantically to get to McQuay in time to save him.

First Class Petty Officer Harold Oleson clutched his friend's wrists to pull him onto the lifeboat, but Clayton kept slipping from his grasp. He repeatedly fell back into the oily black mess.

"Hook your fingers!" Clayton shouted. His life depended on it. Both men hooked their fingers down toward the palms of their hands and locked them with each other. Oleson snaked his friend over into the lifeboat. But First Class Petty Officer Clayton McQuay had not been alone in the oily water. Hundreds of brave men were desperately fighting to stay above the toxic waves as well. It was shortly after 8 a.m. on Sunday, December 7, 1941. They were in the water next to the sinking USS *Oklahoma*, in an area known as Battleship Row. Thousands had become the unwilling victims of the attack on Pearl Harbor, Hawaii.

Clayton McQuay graduated from high school in Charlotte, North Carolina in the spring of 1934. It was during the Depression, and good jobs were tough to find. A recruiter visiting his school talked him into enlisting in the Navy. Twenty-one dollars a month and a steady job sounded sweet.

After training in Norfolk, Virginia, he was assigned to the *Oklahoma*, a 583-foot-long battleship that had been christened on March 23, 1914. Gunner's mate Clayton McQuay served with the crew as they traveled to England, Sweden, Majorca Island, Gibraltar, Spain, and France. The *Oklahoma* transported approximately one-hundred

Americans, evacuated from Spain during the Spanish Revolution, to safety in France.

In December 1941, 26-year-old Clayton McQuay, a ringer for movie star Cary Grant, reveled in the balmy Hawaiian breezes when he wasn't on duty at the deck of the battleship. The U.S. Armed Forces were anticipating and preparing to fight the Japanese, but the opinion was that ships would be somewhat safe from torpedo attack in the 40-foot shallow waters of Pearl Harbor. The military strategists hadn't counted on a slight modification the Japanese made to their torpedo fins, which had previously been ineffective in depths less than 75 feet. The Japanese had been preparing for nearly a year to attack Pearl Harbor.

The Pacific Fleet had been ordered to return to Pearl Harbor on December 5, 1941. Numerous ships, including the *Oklahoma*, had been on maneuvers to find Japanese warships, and the alert was canceled.

On Saturday, December 6, the crew of the *Oklahoma* spent the day firing guns and training. McQuay, as one of the turret captains, was firing a 14" gun from one of the ten gun turrets. After a long day of training, the crew planned to spend Sunday preparing for the Monday morning inspection by the Admiral.

By early Sunday morning the guns were being cleaned, hatches were open, and everywhere sailors were busy scrubbing and polishing. Other than the work ahead, it looked like another perfect day in paradise.

McQuay was in turret number 4 when he felt the ship shudder and a sound similar to dishes rattling. It was just before 8 AM when the Division Officer sounded "General Quarters" and shouted excitedly over the PA system, "All hands man your battle stations and set watertight conditions!" Almost immediately, the loudspeaker came on again. "Hey! Real planes, real bombs! Man your battle stations! This is no—!"

The second torpedo slammed into the hull and exploded. Forty Japanese torpedo planes and forty-nine level bombers launched a full-scale attack on Pearl Harbor, and the Americans were unprepared. While the ships feebly fought the enemy with antiaircraft fire, bombs whistled from the sky, and torpedoes fell to the water with deadly accuracy. As soon as the second torpedo hit the port side of the *Oklahoma*, the great ship began to list.

Clayton was typical of most of the other sailors; he was too busy doing exactly what he had spent seven years training for to worry about dying that day. Men scrambled

160

to their battle stations - the engine rooms, guns, and damage control posts.

Smoke billowed into the sky in angry columns of ugly black, as the Japanese attack planes kept coming and kept coming like a swarm of angry hornets. Three waves over the next two hours continued to wreak destruction. Bombs whistled down and landed with sickening explosions, obliterating everything around them.

Nearby, the *Arizona* had taken a direct hit in the powder magazine, setting off over a million pounds of gunpowder. The mighty battleship exploded into flames and choking black smoke. She broke in two and sank in less than nine minutes. Sadly, 1,177 brave American crewmen of the *Arizona* perished as a result of that awful explosion.

Other battleships along Ford Island were hit as well. Besides the *Oklahoma* and the *Arizona*, the *West Virginia* sank, and the *California, Maryland, Tennessee, Nevada,* and the flagship, the *Pennsylvania,* were all crippled. Of the 394 aircraft on the island, 323 were totally destroyed or damaged.

Clayton McQuay saw the low-flying Japanese planes as they swooped down from the sky. Some were so close he could see the pilots laughing at the devastation. Clayton lost count of the horrendous torpedo hits after the first four.

The ship's twisting metal screeched as men tried to clamber out to safety, gasping for precious air.

As the mortally wounded battleship capsized port-side into the frigid water, a final order was shouted, "Abandon ship!" Clayton jumped into the water, now covered with thousands of gallons of fuel oil. In seven to eight minutes, the ship had capsized, after having taken nine torpedo hits. Water rushed into the ship through the open wounds, trapping crewmen inside the maze of halls and compartments. One hole was a gaping 70 feet long. Everywhere, sailors were desperately trying to save their ship, their comrades, and themselves.

Two seaplanes had been on the deck of the *Oklahoma*. One was pitched upside-down in the water, and Clayton McQuay was among the twenty or so men who struggled to hold onto the slippery wing, hoping they would soon be saved. They were all covered with black oil, stinging their eyes and nostrils. Here and there, fires raged in the flammable oil, now floating everywhere in the once-beautiful harbor, consuming everything and everyone in its path. All they could do was hope to be rescued before they were burned alive. Others were not so lucky. The stranded men looked silently over at the wreck of the mighty *Oklahoma*, her mast now sinking into the mud.

Harold Oleson pulled as many survivors as he could onto the lifeboat. The men got to the fuel docks on Ford Island and took cover under the tables in the mess hall. The whole island vibrated with every new explosion. It would take days to get themselves free of the awful oily mess that covered them. It was the least of their worries.

Even as the Japanese continued their aerial attack, men climbed up onto the capsized ship with cutting torches and immediately set about freeing their comrades. Several men were killed by the acetylene torches used by their liberators. After that disheartening discovery, their rescuers used air chisels. From deep inside the cavernous ship, desperate men hammered out "SOS" with dog wrenches. They would continue for two more days, eventually freeing 31 men. For far too many though, help came too late.

Immediately, Clayton McQuay and Harold Oleson were assigned to a cruiser, the *Helena*. The *Helena* had taken a hit in the fire room, killing 37 men. Clayton got there in time to see the grim removal of bodies.

In spite of the surprise attack, nine Japanese fighters, five torpedo planes, and fifteen dive bombers were shot from the sky. Japanese Commander Mitsuo Fuchida had worn a red shirt on the mission in the event he was shot.

The shirt would camouflage his spilled blood and not discourage the rest of his crew. He survived.

Over 2,395 American servicemen and civilians were killed at the bombing of Pearl Harbor. Another 1,178 were wounded. Over 400 of those casualties were aboard the *Oklahoma*.

On March 8, 1943, the *Oklahoma* was uprighted using shore-based electric winches. It was then that a terrible discovery was made. Four men trapped in the watertight compartments of the storeroom had survived for nineteen days after the attack on Pearl Harbor. They had even changed into their winter uniforms, and kept a calendar that documented the desperate days until they perished.

The hull was patched enough to float her, and the former battleship *Oklahoma* was sold to a razor blade company in December, 1946. Five months later, she was pulled by a tugboat towards the coast of Washington. Enroute, a storm sunk the ship, nearly taking the tugboat in the process. The tow line was "cut" and the tugboat was spared. It was an undignified ending for the mighty ship.

The *Utah* and *Arizona* remain where they sank, permanent memorials to the men who may be lost, but will never be forgotten.

Clayton McQuay spent twenty years in the Navy and retired as a Chief Petty Officer. Harold Oleson, his friend from Belle Plain, Kansas, died later in the war while serving on a cruiser. His vessel had been hit, and he was helping to extinguish a fire on deck, trying vainly to keep the flames away from the bombs and other munitions stored there. But the crew's efforts were insufficient and one bomb exploded, blowing off Oleson's legs. Another brave American was dead. Oleson's death continues to be a painful loss for Mr. McQuay.

Clayton McQuay and his wife Frances are prominent residents of the Big Cove community in Madison County, Alabama. He still gets emotional when he remembers his lost friends, and perhaps even more so, as the years go by.

No words or gesture will ever adequately convey the profound sense of gratitude we Americans feel for the brave men and women who fought for our country. We can never compensate for their tremendous sacrifices.

Sadly, in June 2002, Mr. McQuay died in a car accident just a few weeks after this story was published. He is missed very much.

Maria Donnell, James Webb Smith Donnell

Fortunes Lost

A protective canopy of trees filters light onto a small patch of ground near a cotton field. Shadows in and around the uneven ground cover reveal indentations of graves. Carefully arranged piles of rocks dot the area, crude monuments to the loved ones below.

It is a slave cemetery, and in the center is a six-foot marker at the head of one grave. The slave's name was Fortune, and it was said that fortune is exactly what he brought to his master, the wealthy owner of two plantations. His master lost everything in the war, and his own grave was unmarked for 125 years after his death.

James (Jim) Webb Smith Donnell, born in 1820, was a descendant of the MacDonalds killed at the Glencoe Massacre in Scotland in 1692. A MacDonald had already come to America before the vicious slaughter, and his descendants fought the English again in the American Revolution. His father's pioneer family came into Alabama while it was still a territory.

Jim Donnell acquired a 2400 acre Lawrence County plantation from his wife's aunt, near the community known today as Town Creek, Alabama. He named his plantation Seclusion and built a two-story home of the finest materials. The wonderful parties and dances held at Seclusion were well attended. Large pocket doors were opened to accommodate the crowds. Ladies' party dresses and petticoats swirled as laughing couples danced through the length of the entire house by candlelight.

With all his inherited wealth, Jim remained an ambitious man. He dabbled in politics, supported local schools, and successfully ran two plantations. He had numerous children and loved his family very much. His letters indicated an affection toward the family slaves as well. When he told his wife to give his love to his children, he also asked to be remembered to the slaves, named individually.

Not much is known about the slave named Fortune, except that Donnell thought much of him. Historians agree that it was probably Fortune that Donnell referred to in his letters as "Fort," a man he obviously trusted highly. One source believed that he was Donnell's coachman. Family members say that Fortune had a brick home to live in, while other slaves lived in frame houses. What we do know is that Donnell grieved over the death of Fortune and he erected two markers in his memory. One is at the foot of his grave, and a much larger one at the head. Both markers bear the same inscription, "Fortune...Died February 1859...To the virtues and excellencies of a faithful servant this testimony is erected by his master, J.W.S. Donnell."

Cedar trees once flanked the straight narrow lane that led to the imposing Donnell home. The house was fairly far from present Highway 72, but probably close enough to be seen from the road. Cotton grew out of the rocky soil, and a small lake formed where the red clay was dug out to make bricks. Chips of those bricks still litter the low area where the now-shallow lake bottom is cultivated with cotton. At that time, there was a dense forest on Donnell's property as well. Donnell cut and sold fire wood to the Memphis and Charleston Railroad. Preserved letters document the frustrating and acrimonious relationship between Seclusion's overseer and railroad officials. Donnell's green wood was blamed on several occasions for causing the trains to run late. Other letters complain that it was not cut to exact specifications. Still others complain that the stacked wood was too close to the tracks, and then not close enough.

The spacious family home had a long porch across the entire front, supported by pine columns. The main two front rooms were 22 by 24 feet, and the back rooms were 16 by 22 feet. The stairway was ornately carved and thought to have been imported from England. Upstairs were four large bedrooms, an apartment, and a sleeping porch for hot summer nights. No doubt the many Donnell children enjoyed watching the fireflies from that porch, as the crickets serenaded them to sleep. The house had eight fireplaces, four were seven-and-a-half feet wide. The downstairs baseboards were an incredible two-and-a-half feet high.

Jim's grandfather, James Webb Smith, once gave him 1,000 acres of the family farmland in Tennessee, but was infuriated when Jim sold it. Despite a lack of sentimentality, Jim had good business sense.

Prosperity would be short-lived, as discussions of secession became heated and hostile. The only known photograph of Jim Donnell and his wife was taken at about the time the war started. He was a very handsome man, but the worried look on his face did not hide his concern about what lie ahead.

War was declared, and neighbors squared off against each other. Though many, including Jim, did all they could to prevent the schism, when the inevitable happened, men who had once been friends, were now bitter enemies.

North Alabama was taken by surprise by the Union Army in April, 1862. Jim Donnell was a Southern sympathizer and before long, he and others like him became prey to soldiers on both sides who confiscated horses, mules, cotton, and food.

The South suffered relentlessly during the War Between the States. As a Major in the 22nd Alabama Infantry, Jim's son Robert fought in some of the bloodiest battles: Shiloh, Franklin, Chickamauga, and others.

Jim's wife Maria was pregnant with their 13th child during the war. She stayed with the young children in the Athens, Alabama home known as Pleasant Hill, which Jim inherited when his father died in 1855. Jim and their oldest daughter were stranded at Seclusion, unable to return to Athens because there was an outstanding warrant for his arrest. As a Southern sympathizer, he was a wanted man. Union soldiers entered the Donnell home in Athens with orders to arrest Jim and his son Robert, who was still fighting in the Confederate Army. While searching the premises, the soldiers filled their pockets with whatever souvenirs they wanted, and a Union soldier stole the family silver. During the Union occupation of Athens, the soldiers camped out on the grounds of the Donnell home and used the home for their offices.

Maria tried to cope with the tenuous situation, but she was terrified for her family. She kept her children inside, and away from the invading army during what became known as the Sack of Athens. Union General Ivan Turchin announced that he would close his eyes for two hours, practically ordering his men to plunder the city. They did so with relish. Union General Mitchel later wrote to the people of Athens from Huntsville, informing them that whatever damage caused by individual marauders was not authorized by the Army, and therefore not his concern. The destruction encouraged by Turchin earned him a court martial, a trial, and a guilty verdict.

Maria's brother, John Haywood Jones, had just moved into a magnificent new Athens home, not far from his sister. The Union soldiers stormed his house, doing an extensive amount of damage throughout. They cut hams from the smokehouse, and sliced them with their swords on top of the family piano. Official records of the war described how the Yankees slept on the family's fine satin sheets, without removing their muddy boots and spurs first.

Maria's desperate letters to Jim pleaded with him to come home to help her. The servants stopped working, but refused to leave the plantation even after they were asked to. As indicated in Maria's letters, slaves invited the Union soldiers to live with them in their cabins, and with so many extra people to feed, the food supply was soon gone. Two servants agreed to plant a garden only if Maria would sign a contract giving them half of everything they could grow. She agreed, but they lost interest and abandoned the field. If that wasn't enough, 16-year-old daughter Nannie died during the occupation.

During this time, Major Robert Donnell wrote a letter to his mother, Maria. "...Our rations are very short indeed, but I am willing to live on acorns for seven years or longer to gain my freedom and independence...We adopt for our motto an old saying of one of the Revolutionary fathers of '76 that 'Resistance to tyrants is obedience to God.' I hope the people of Athens will not despair or give up. You must encourage the desponding and vacillating; tell them to trust to our valor and to God." He included messages for the servants, "...Tell Jack and Cesar that my confidence in them is unbounded..."

Jim Donnell grappled with a different set of problems in Lawrence County. The Confederate soldiers took 15 bales of cotton for fortification, then abandoned them when they could not transport them. He wrote to Union General

Ormsby Mitchel, commanding officer during the Union occupation, asking permission to retrieve them. Whether or not he got them back is not known. The Union soldiers confiscated horses, foodstuffs, and over 40 mules from Seclusion. Jim had already loaned 70 bales of cotton to the Confederacy for fortifications and the Federals burned some 500 bales during the course of the war. Indeed, the South had been turned into a smoldering wasteland. Plantations were burned out and abandoned. Fences were torn down, fields were filled with weeds, and the people were gloomy and subjugated.

By the end of the war, Jim's wealth was gone. On November 27, 1865, James Webb Smith Donnell signed his name to an oath of loyalty to the United States government. As a member of Major General Daniel Harvey Hill's staff, his son, Major Robert Donnell, oversaw the surrender of Confederate forces in Bentonville, North Carolina. He then returned home to help his father recover from his losses and rebuild what was left.

Jim tried to pay his enormous debts by working the fields with former slaves now known as freedmen, who worked for wages. Those who owed him money could not pay him, and Seclusion yielded only three bales of cotton in the last year Donnell owned it. Finally, Seclusion and

Pleasant Hill in Athens were offered up for auction in 1867 to pay the debts and high taxes.

Jim Donnell's frustration poured into his letters as he tried to continue farming to support his family. He was victimized several more times as the carpetbaggers and marauders took over and terrorized the demoralized Southerners. In despair, Jim signed bankruptcy papers in 1869. He died a few years later at the age of 56, leaving several young children for his widow to raise alone. Some of his children, among them Major Robert, moved to Texas to start over. Others drifted in different directions and the family eventually lost track of them.

Over the years, the beautiful plantation home near Fortune's grave was divided into apartments and fell into disrepair. The decaying symbol of Southern wealth was finally torn down in the mid-1940s. Salvageable pieces were sold off.

Today the farm once known as Seclusion is still producing cotton. The family that now owns it proudly maintains the slave cemetery, guarding and protecting it as a historical reminder of Alabama's past. The bell that once rang to call the slaves in from the field is about the only remnant of the lives that once graced that era. Except, of

Jacquelyn Procter Gray

course, for a headstone in memory of the slave named Fortune.

Unpardonable Sin

Oscar Hundley didn't worry much about what other people thought of him. He briefly attended a northern Ivy League university, but left because the "Yankee climate" didn't suit him. Oscar was outspoken and not afraid of controversy. When he built his Huntsville, Alabama home at 401 Madison Street in 1900, it was the first private home in town with indoor plumbing. After an impressive career as an attorney, he was appointed as a Federal district judge for North Alabama. Oscar then made a decision that was so unspeakable and shocking, that it ended his impressive career in politics. Oscar lived his life very publicly; his friends adored him and his enemies hated him. But no one could ever accuse Oscar of being a bore!

Oscar's grandparents came to Alabama from Virginia. One source reports that Dr. John Henderson Hundley purchased 160 acres in Madison County in the year 1815.

John and his wife Malinda Robinson Hundley built a 12-room plantation home near Mooresville to raise their family. While some descendants refer to the old home site as Hundley Hill, others know it as Hundley Hall. Perhaps the disagreement stems from where their recollections linger - the old home place itself or the grounds, which include the nearby family cemetery. Buttercups emerge amid the bricks and rubble of the home's foundation. Among the graveyard's toppled and decaying headstones, a glorious groundcover of periwinkle still blooms each spring. Both sites retain a quiet beauty. Now owned by a prominent Mooresville resident, the property is located on the south side of I-565, near the Greenbrier exit.

The view that spans over the large cotton field probably hasn't changed significantly since the Hundleys celebrated their lives and mourned their tragedies there, though now it is mostly enjoyed by the cows that graze the land, oblivious to the echoes of the past.

A cave, called a rock house, was on the family property near the Hundley homesite. According to a story handed down in the Hundley family, a slave exploring the cave found a skull, presumed to be Indian, with a projectile lodged in the bone. The souvenir was too distasteful to display inside the home, so the gruesome artifact was placed on the porch.

Accounts of the family's years on Hundley Hill at times seem written in tears. John and Malinda's oldest son,

Oscar, was 25 when he died in 1852 of unspecified causes. His nephew, the subject of this story, was named for him.

The prosperous life enjoyed by the family came to a crashing end with the Civil War. Three sons, William, Daniel, and Orville, enlisted in the Confederate cause in Mooresville. Major William Hundley was chasing Yankees along the Tennessee River one night when he was knocked off his horse by a low-hanging branch. His skull was fractured. William was taken back to Hundley Hill to spend his last hours enveloped in the comfort of his loving family. Instead of succumbing to his wound, he recovered sufficiently and traveled to Atlanta to resume fighting.

On March 31, 1864, William was in his tent preparing for the day ahead. A soldier came to call him to breakfast, but found Hundley dead. He had one boot on, and was in the act of pulling on the other which he had fallen on top of. A blood clot to the brain took him at the age of 29. William Hundley was brought back to Hundley Hill for burial, and promoted posthumously to the rank of lieutenant colonel.

Daniel Hundley was captured in Georgia and sent to the Union prisoner of war camp at Johnson's Island near Sandusky, Ohio. Along his journey to the Union prison, Daniel implored his captors to treat him with respect by announcing to them, "I trust I am among gentlemen."

In Daniel's diary, published after the war as *Prison Echoes of the Great Rebellion,* he described the horrible conditions endured by the starving prisoners. He was surprised one day to see his brother Orville arrive at Johnson's Island as a prisoner.

Col. Daniel Hundley's dramatic escape from Johnson's Island and subsequent recapture were graphically recorded in his published diary.

The surviving brothers came back from the war to find much of the family's wealth depleted. Judge Richard Hundley, retired presiding circuit judge of Morgan County, is a direct descendant of Col. William Hundley. He recounted several interesting family anecdotes. After the war, Daniel bought a new carriage and four matching horses. He apparently felt that his status still called for some luxury and semblance of class distinction. Daniel's brother Orville was the only Hundley who came out of the war with some fortune intact. In one local who's who publication, he submitted his occupation as "Capitalist."

Shortly after the war, the Hundleys either sold or lost the home site known as Hundley Hill/Hall. Some of the graves were moved to Maple Hill Cemetery in Huntsville, while others remain under the protection of the old cedar trees that still surround the old home site. Remnants of the house - bricks and door hinges - still litter the vicinity of the plantation house that eventually burned.

The second Oscar Hundley, the subject of this story, was born in Limestone County in 1854, probably at Hundley Hill. He was named for his father Orville's older brother who died just two years earlier. He attended college "up north" for a short period of time, but according to a family story, he returned to the South because the Yankee climate didn't agree with him. Oscar was educated at Phillips Exeter Academy, Marietta College, and graduated from Vanderbilt University before he returned to Alabama to practice law in 1878.

While serving as city attorney from 1882 to 1884, Oscar wrote the Code of Ordinances of the City of Huntsville. In addition to serving eleven years in the state legislature, Hundley was the division counsel for the Nashville, Chattanooga, and St. Louis Railway for nearly 20 years. He ran against, and was defeated by, Gen. Joseph Wheeler for congress from the Eighth Alabama district. Oscar was also an advocate for the advancement of public education, an endeavor considered rather frivolous at a time when cotton pickers and mill workers were in such demand.

Oscar's first wife Annie died in 1893. Newspaper accounts report that she was in Waukesha, Wisconsin when she died, perhaps unexpectedly. After Annie's death, he married Bossie O'Brien, a Catholic girl significantly younger than Oscar, whose family knew future president Teddy Roosevelt. After having descended from several generations of devoted supporters of the Disciples of Christ, Oscar became a devout Catholic himself.

It wasn't Oscar's opinionated personality, or religious conversion that caused his first cousin, William Hundley, to insist that Oscar's name never be spoken in his household again. It was because Oscar did something so scandalous, that it ultimately prevented him from being confirmed by the Senate for his appointment as Federal district judge for North Alabama and ultimately ended his political career.

In 1896, Democrat Oscar Hundley became a Republican.

In her book "Changing Huntsville 1890-1899," Elizabeth Humes Chapman described the party switch incident as well as the public perception of such an act of treason. "To be born a Democrat and become a Republican was treachery. It was almost as disgraceful as being divorced in the nineties. The person was not acknowledged in his family. He was mentioned with apology and omitted from the family will."

She further described the reaction of Charles Lane, editor of *The Evening Tribune* and *Weekly Tribune*, to Oscar's decision.   Ms. Chapman wrote, "After Mr. Hundley's change of parties he was awarded a foreign appointment. Mr. Lane then said editorially, "For once we are for Oscar. We hear he has a foreign appointment. We're glad, and the foreigner it is the better we'll like it."

After the Senate twice refused to confirm Hundley's nomination, he resigned as district judge in 1909. He sold his Huntsville home the same year, and moved to Birmingham to practice law. He and Bossie lived in a spacious mansion on Niazuma Avenue. Instead of living a life of exile and shame however, Oscar easily became a scion of Birmingham society. He even became well known for his expertise on the dance floor. Whatever Oscar did, he did well.

The Hundley plot at Maple Hill Cemetery contains graves moved from the Hundley Hill plantation, as well as the more contemporary graves of the 1900's. Oscar's first wife Annie is buried there along with his parents, the uncle he was named for, his uncle William, who was killed in the war, and other family members with their own interesting stories.

Oscar Hundley died in 1921 at the age of 67. Though his actions were considered scandalous and outrageous at the time, they would hardly make the news in today's papers. Oscar was indeed a man ahead of his time.

Photograph of Judge Oscar R. Hundley, made shortly after appointment to the office of Judge of the Northern District of Ala., by President Theodore Roosevelt.

Jacquelyn Procter Gray

The Silver Spoon

The silver spoon is pockmarked and bent. In spite of its worn and fragile condition, it represents nearly two centuries of life, death, heartache, and war. The triumphs and tragedies of the Southern family this spoon represents, have been carefully preserved through descendants who still carry the spirit of their pioneer forefathers.

The spoon was hammered out of a silver coin by a slave who was trained as a silversmith nearly 200 years ago. It bears the monogram "RAD," the initials of Robert Donnell.

The Donnells lived in North Carolina, and Robert's father fought in the Battle of Guilford Court House during the Revolutionary War. The Donnells then traveled to Wilson County, Tennessee in the 1790s to start a new life, but lost what few possessions they had during an Indian attack. William Donnell died of fever when his son Robert was 15, leaving him the head of a struggling family.

Robert received God's calling and became a Cumberland Presbyterian minister in the frontier territory now known as Alabama. He rode horseback to new settlements, and established churches that still exist. He was so well-loved that parents named their sons after him and the practice continued over 100 years after his death.

Robert married the daughter of a Tennessee politician, and possibly his marriage to Ann Eliza Smith was the occasion for which the silver spoon was created.

While Robert traveled the harsh frontier spreading the word of God, Ann was home having babies. They lost four children in infancy, and perhaps Ann used this silver spoon to stir her tea as she spent many hours alone in worry. Only their son James survived infancy, and he was just eight when his frail mother died.

After Robert Donnell's death in 1855, son James Webb Smith Donnell, his wife Maria, and their children moved into the home built by Robert in Athens, Alabama. Maria may have used the silver spoon to stir cornbread batter while the family anxiously waited for news of their son, who wore the gray uniform in the Civil War.

When the Union Army captured Athens, the soldiers camped on the grounds of the Donnell home. Sixteen-year-old daughter, Nannie, was sick with scarlet fever. When her mother asked the soldiers to keep their music down during her daughter's illness, she received a surly reply that her daughter could go to heaven listening to Yankee music.

Nannie died. Her mother was pregnant at the time, and when her baby girl was born a few months later, the child was named in memory of the sister she never knew.

The silver spoon may have been dropped behind the wood cook stove or perhaps hidden away by one of the children. The Union soldiers "confiscated" all the silver from the Donnell home, and the matching flatware disappeared.

The war finally ended in 1865, and Jim Donnell's son came home after fighting in such bloody battles as Shiloh, Chickamauga, and Franklin. Though he fought to keep the family and possessions together, Jim lost everything, and he died brokenhearted. Life in the South during Reconstruction was difficult and violent. Several of the grown children moved to Texas in search of a better life.

The younger Donnell children struggled to stay together in the home built by their maternal grandparents in the nearby village of Greenbrier, Alabama. The silver spoon went to Greenbrier too, and perhaps it was used to scoop dirt in the garden by a little boy named William Hundley, the younger son of Nannie Donnell Hundley.

William grew up and went to France wearing an American uniform in World War I. He wrote a letter of comfort to his mother Nannie, "I will keep straight and sober in all of my journey, and in the end, I will be a better man in every respect."

A flag with one star was displayed in the window of the Hundley home, a proud symbol that their son fought for America. William must have been overwhelmed on his first trip away from home. He was sent to war-torn France. The long sleepless nights spent worrying about William seemed endless, and Nannie may have used the silver spoon to dish up turnip greens to celebrate William's safe return home.

William married Ellen Stewart a few years after the war, and they raised their family in Greenbrier. Hobos riding the rails in front of the house frequently stopped by the kitchen for a snack in the middle of the night, eating Ellen's pies and chicken she had planned for Sunday dinner.

Their middle child was a reckless, fast-living teen who drove too fast and stayed out too late. Ellen worried about him, and she may have used the silver spoon to stir her coffee as she waited for him to come home.

One spring night in 1947, her worst fears were realized. Billy Don missed a curve and lay unconscious by the side of the road for hours, until someone discovered him and called for help. For three days, Billy Don lingered in a coma. William stayed at the hospital by his son's side.

Ellen waited the entire time outside in the car. She couldn't bear to see her son, broken and bleeding.

They say that the funeral procession went as far as the eye could see, and the high school senior was laid to rest in the middle of the cotton field in Greenbrier, alongside his father's ancestors. His mother, too distraught to attend the funeral, quietly packed up his pictures and belongings, and in her grief, she rarely spoke of her only son.

On a hot August day in 1960, William was sweeping the floor and fell dead of a heart attack. His daughter, Peggy, and her family, had just left to drive to their home out west. He was silently grieving when his heart simply stopped. State police stopped his daughter, and broke the tragic news.

William was buried next to his son Billy Don, and Ellen was alone in the big house once filled with several generations of family and laughing children.

Twenty-three years later, Ellen was found lying on the floor with a broken hip. The house was locked up, still furnished, waiting for the day that she could come back to her beloved home, but she never did. She remained in the hospital for five years before her death, and she was also laid to rest in the cotton field with her husband and son.

The silver spoon, considered by some to be old and worn, is a treasure of pure beauty. With care, it will survive through many more generations of the descendants of Robert Donnell, and remain a symbol of renewal.

As for the man who once held the coin in his hands and skillfully turned it into this spoon that has withstood the ages, I wonder if he had any idea that one day his descendants would be free of the chains that once bound him to another human being, and that his own handiwork would be appreciated by so many generations long after his name was forgotten.

The Long Road to Victory

On January 17, 1945, Mrs. Eola Mills received a telegram. "We regret to inform you that your son, George Mills,..." The blood drained from her face as she read the dreaded words. She did not want a gold star in the window of her Decatur, Alabama home. "...has been reported missing in action since 18 December..." She read those words again - "missing in action." At least there was hope.

Mrs. Mills was afraid for her son George, a handsome young man with brown eyes and hair. The Decatur High School graduate, one of eight children, had been a salesman at Forbes Piano Company. One day, a woman who worked at the draft board across the street leaned out of the second story window and called out to him.

"Just got word you'll be drafted on Wednesday!"

It was May, 1942, and George wasn't surprised. He hedged his bets by volunteering on Monday with two of his buddies, hoping he could serve his time in the military with them. It was a nice thought.

After basic training at Camp Livingston, Louisiana, George was sent to Florida for amphibious training. He next went to Pickett, Virginia to learn how to scale cliffs. He was a gung-ho fighter when he shipped out of Camp Miles Standish, just outside of Boston, on a troop transport bound for England. The date was October 8, 1943.

George was a member of the 28th Infantry Division. Elements of the 28th traced back to the year 1747. They became known as the "Keystone" troops in World War I, where they helped rescue the "Lost Battalion" in the Meuse-Argonne offensive. The red keystone insignia was approved by the War Department in 1918, and was nicknamed the "Bloody Bucket" by the Germans who suffered tremendously under the onslaught of the 28th Infantry Division during World War II.

The convoy of transport ships landed in Bristol, England. George spent eight months at his first assignment in South Wales. He and a friend took leave to spend a few days in London, while lodging at no cost at the Marble Arch Hotel. One night they were enjoying beer in a pub when they heard the dreaded sound of a German V-1 rocket flying overhead. The rocket engine made an intermittent whirring sound, and as long as the sound of the engine could be heard, everyone knew they were safe. But when the whirring stopped, the people around them instantly froze, because they knew it would land close, if not directly on them. On this night, the rocket landed a block away, sucking all the windows out of the pub. When the shards of flying glass stopped tinkling around them, George and his friend turned to the barkeep and ordered another round.

The 28th Infantry Division also spent time in Tidworth, England, before following the 29th Infantry Division across the English Channel to France. It was the job of the 29th to clear barbed wire and debris, remove booby traps, and generally make the beachhead ready for the 29th to come in with tanks, trucks, and heavy mortar. The 29th Infantry arrived at Omaha Beach on June 6, 1944 - D-Day!

George's Division landed at Omaha Beach in July. The destruction left from the D-Day Invasion was evident everywhere. The young men had been anxious to get into battle and fight the Germans. While still aboard their transport, they looked around in the waters to see sunken ships everywhere from the battle. Their enthusiasm shriveled as the smell of death rose up to greet them.

They fought through the hedgerows of Normandy - curious barriers planted by farmers in lieu of fences. The tall hedgerows became natural defensive positions for German snipers who fought relentlessly for their failing cause. After losing too many men to sniper fire, the Americans flushed them out with flame throwers.

By the first of August, German troops in Western France faced fifteen U.S. divisions. The British and Canadians were closing in from the northeast, and the German stronghold was crumbling. Still, they would not give up.

George Mills and the men of Company E fought through the countryside of France, liberating small towns and villages as they made their way to Paris. Outside of Paris, they held back to let the Free French in to finish wiping out the German snipers, all that was left of the German occupation. The French needed to have the victory for themselves, as well as the satisfaction of liberating their own city.

On August 29, 1944, the 28th Infantry Division marched in the famous Liberation Parade on the Champs-Elysees. The French civilians crowded the streets and cheered their liberators. French girls rushed to kiss the soldiers, and bouquets of flowers were thrown from the crowds. Like many of his fellow American soldiers, George thought the sentiment was foolish - the war was still far from over.

On September 10, the 109th and 110th regiments marched into Germany with no resistance. They were the first infantry division to enter Germany. Ahead of them lay the seemingly impossible task of breaking through the Dragon's Teeth of the Siegfried Line on German's western border, and the destruction of hundreds of German gun emplacements known as pillboxes.

By now, the American GIs were becoming hardened to the consequences of war. Most of their time was spent looking for artillery and mines, digging foxholes, and watching for traps left by retreating Germans. They had seen too many senseless deaths, and they were sick of it.

By October, they had arrived in the Hurtgen Forest, unaware of the blood bath that lay ahead.

The Hurtgen Forest was situated southeast of Aachen. It consisted of thick woods and difficult terrain. George Mills noticed that even at noon, it was as dark as night inside the forest. The German High Command instructed the Nazis to maintain control of this area *at all costs*. Originally, the Americans planned to attack the Germans in the Hurtgen Forest on October 31, but inclement weather interfered. Orders were issued to hold the Vossenack-

Schmidt Line, capture Steckenborn, remove resistance north of Rollesbroich, and capture the 5th Armored Division.

After three days of poor weather conditions, the assault got underway at 9 a.m. on November 2. Three American regiments entered the dense stand of forest pines. At first the Americans held the upper hand, but by November 4, the German Army had rallied and the 112th Infantry began to falter. Platoons of Companies K and L were overrun, and by November 9, the German commander called for the Americans to surrender. Eighteen battalions of American artillery gave him the answer he didn't want.

Throughout the few days of fighting in the Hurtgen Forest, 5,700 Americans were killed. The massive pines of the forest were left twisted and splintered, and the grounds were nearly impassable. German loss was high too; it was estimated that 4,000 were killed and 1,100 prisoners taken, while the Americans held firm.

With the worst of the fighting behind them, the 28th Infantry was sent to Fuhren. Another horrendous fight lay ahead of them. It was known as the Battle of the Bulge.

The morning of December 16, 1944 was cold and overcast. Clouds hung low and thick, and George was in Walls loading up jeeps with buckets of pancakes, syrup, and sausage to take to the troops at Fuhren for their

197

breakfast. Suddenly, the sky lit up with German rockets and artillery. The approximately 200 men of Company E were surrounded - the 5th Panzer Division was on their left flank and the 373rd Vanguard Division was on their right. The German assault was code-named "Watch on the Rhine," and the Allies faced 38 German divisions who arrived along the 50-mile front through a cover of thick fog.

Headquarters for Company E were set up in the Betzen House, an ancient manor house three stories tall. George climbed into a Jeep to go to headquarters to see if he could help somehow. The telephone lines were cut and the Germans kept up their steady assault. Strategically, they had the advantage, as their tanks were on a hill overlooking the houses in Fuhren, where the Americans had taken cover. By 2:25 p.m., contact with Company E was lost, and with the heavy fog, they had no hope of receiving air support.

The soldiers inside the Betzen House were running out of ammunition, and two Jeeps and a tank sent to replenish their supplies were knocked out. The fierce fight continued throughout the night of December 16 with no let-up. The Germans hammered away at the Americans throughout December 17 and 18. Holes were blown through the north wall by bazookas, and Germans came in with flame throwers. George received a shrapnel wound to his face, but there was no time to worry about it. Finally, on the evening of December 18, they were left with six rounds of ammunition. The captain in command announced that they had no choice but to surrender.

The civilians, who had taken refuge in the Betzen root cellar, were ordered by the Germans to leave the building first. The first man out was the mayor. He was immediately shot. Along with the other civilians, fifteen-year-old Adolphe Betzen, heir to the manor house, and his younger sister Elsie, walked out into the frigid night. George worried about their safety; they were so innocent.

By 9:30 p.m., the civilians had all surrendered. The Americans disassembled their weapons and scattered the pieces before their surrender to the German army. They were afraid, and did not know what lay ahead for them. The icy wind was bitter, and snow was falling. As the 200 cold American soldiers, now prisoners-of war, walked away from Betzen, they heard the rumble of the U.S. artillery behind them, destroying what was left of the town of Fuhren.

Sergeant George Mills started walking that freezing December night, unaware that he would not stop for the next five months. They spent two nights at Stalag IVB for fingerprinting and processing. It was there that the officers, non-commissioned officers, and privates were separated and sent in different directions. George wrote a letter to his mother, asking for socks and food. By the time she finally got the letter, he was long gone. Next, they were sent to Stalag VIIIA for two nights, and it was there that they could hear the Russian artillery advancing in their direction. Their German guards turned the prisoners around to march toward the American front.

On Christmas Day, 1944, the prisoners were next to a railroad yard when American planes came in to attack the trains and railroad line. They strafed the boxcars. Sadly, they killed many American prisoners, members of the 101st Airborne Division.

At the time of his capture, George weighed 190 pounds. The Germans had little food to spare, so he and the other prisoners of war struggled to survive by foraging. Occasionally they had potatoes to eat, and a loaf of bread would be shared by eight men. George made a pact with his friend, Andy McLaughlin from Oxford, Ohio, that whatever food they were able to steal would be divided with the other.

One night, as the prisoners slept in a brickyard building, George woke up and smelled the smoke of a lit cigarette. He walked over and through the sleeping prisoners to find the source of the smoke: a Camel cigarette held by a medic. George offered to buy the cigarette from him, but the medic refused to either sell or give him one.

"If you don't sell me one, I'll take it from you," he told the medic.

Under those conditions, the medic reconsidered. George paid him $41 for a single cigarette and he shared it with his pal Andy. The two emaciated men became drunk from the nicotine, and even burned their fingers trying to get every last puff of tobacco.

George's weight plummeted down to 120 pounds. The number of prisoners, which at one time may have been as high as 6,000 as they combined forces with other marching prisoners, dwindled due to dysentery, starvation, and freezing. Many suffered from frostbite. They died as they walked, and their comrades could not stop to bury them. The prisoners were infested with lice, and George once traded his sweater with a German woman for a bucket of potatoes. When he held the sweater up to the sunlight, it appeared to be alive with the movement of lice. He watched as the woman began to unravel the sweater, forcing thousands of lice to scatter everywhere, so she could use the yarn to knit socks.

No matter how they tried to avoid it, the men obsessed about food. They vowed not to talk about it, but when they stopped to rest, the conversation soon turned to a masochistic game of naming candy bars, or some other food group that made them that much hungrier. The German guards were not fed much better. They were old men - all of the stronger young men had been sent to fight. The guards could see, as well as the prisoners, that the Third Reich could not survive much longer.

One evening, as the prisoners slept in a farmer's barn, George heard a noise on the other side of the barn wall. He and Andy McLaughlin loosened a board and saw the most glorious sight - a milk cow! George held his helmet under the cow's udder as his friend, who had fortunately grown up on a farm, milked her. They went back several times in the night to get more milk, and when the farmer came the next morning, he was angry to find that his cow was dry. He yelled at the cow, then yelled at the German guards.

The prisoners were marched in a strange random pattern throughout the countryside. Just as they set up camp one night, one of the soldiers who had suffered terribly from dysentery, died. The Americans asked if they could take his body out of the camp to bury him. The captors relented, and several of the Germans went to keep an eye on them. To the surprise of the Americans, a German bugler began to play "taps." Other Germans fired a volley for the dead American. It was a totally unexpected, but touching tribute from the enemy.

The Americans were now receiving occasional messages that the war was nearly over. George never knew where the messages came from, but he knew it had to be true because the front had moved and their guards were starving too. On April 13, 1945, four Americans in a half-track drove up to the marching prisoners. With them was a command car carrying four more Americans. The prisoners thought they looked strange with their fat faces. They brought news that the prisoners of war were now free to go.

The lice-infested, sick, and tired men rallied enough strength to jump and shout, and hug each other. Their will to live, the only thing that kept them alive, had not been in vain.

The freed Americans were trucked to an airfield. Instead of prisoners of war, they were finally heroes. Their clothing was removed and gassed to kill the lice, and they were sprayed with DDT and sent for a long-awaited shower.

That night, George and Andy looked up the hill to see a tent with a line of men standing in front of it. George convinced Andy it was a chow line, and they sneaked up to watch. They asked Air Force personnel if they could get in line, too. George held his stainless steel tray in front of the man dishing out meat. After the server gave him one piece of meat, George remained, staring at the man. He gave him another, and then another. George repeated this scene all the way down the line and his plate was heaped over, nearly too heavy for the weakened man to carry. He and Andy ate every morsel. Their bellies were soon swollen, and they asked if they could return for breakfast. Of course they were invited back.

Andy threw up all night, his body unaccustomed to the large quantity of relatively-rich food. He told George he couldn't make it back up for breakfast, but when George got up to be in the chow line at 4:30 a.m., Andy told him to wait for him!

After a short stay in LaHavre, France, George was sent on a transport ship back to Camp Miles Standish. They were half-way across the ocean on May 8, when they received word that Germany had surrendered. They were euphoric, but George's thoughts went to their comrades who had not lived to share their victory.

George arrived by bus in his hometown of Decatur, Alabama at 5 a.m. No one was there to meet him because his family had no idea what time he was expected. He walked from the bus station to his home on Sherman Street and opened the door. His mother, father, and sister all screamed in surprise as he walked in. Even though he was thin and ragged, his pit bull recognized his voice and nearly tore the screen door apart trying to get to him.

George Mills gained 60 pounds his first month home. He ate everything he could get his hands on, and it all tasted good. After his discharge from the Army, he went back to Decatur and back to his job at Forbes Music. George kept in touch with about 30 of the former prisoners, but as time went on, many of them began to lose track of each other. His friendship with Andy McLaughlin and Martin Slaughter remained extremely close, until their recent deaths. When asked if it was painful to get together with the former prisoners, knowing that their common link was the shared months of horror, George responded that the ordeal had made them closer than brothers.

George receives a Christmas card every year from Adolphe and Elsie Betzen, the brother and sister who were forced from their manor house the night George was captured. Their home was rebuilt and restored, and is now a bed-and-breakfast. On display inside the house is a large stainless steel bucket with "Co. E" stenciled on it. It was one of the buckets that contained breakfast that December day in 1944.

George and his wife Charlie, a native of Austinville, live on Highway 31 South in Decatur, in the same house they've occupied since 1956. Much has changed around their home, traffic and businesses surround them. But few of the thousands of people that drive past his home every day realize how close they've come to a true American hero. George's walls are covered with citations and medals from the French and American governments - small payment for what was given and what is owed to men like George, Andy, Martin, and the millions of others who sacrificed so much for us.

Mollie Walton - The Maven of Mooresville

Mollie Walton was an eccentric spinster, rumored to be the richest woman in Limestone County, Alabama. In a fit of anger, she cut her closest relative out of her will. For the next one hundred years, her unusual will would spawn several lawsuits and allegations of criminal activity. Yet, for all the controversy caused by Mollie Walton and her will, neither her grave nor her will can today be located.

Mollie Walton's hometown of Mooresville, Alabama is a quiet, picturesque community not known for scandal. Located between the north Alabama towns of Decatur and Huntsville, it is barely large enough for a post office. Mooresville exudes Southern charm and hospitality, and it even served as the temporary residence of two future presidents.

After William Woodroof was killed in 1814, his wealthy widow Elizabeth married Edmond Walton. She already had a young son named James. The three of them came to Limestone County from Virginia, and Walton used his new wife's considerable inheritance to buy a large tract of land which they named Oakwood Plantation. Three children were born to the couple, a son who died as an infant, an attractive daughter who died at age 22, and finally, Mary Ann. Mollie, as she was known to her friends, was born in 1829 at Oakwood Plantation.

Edmond Walton was a shrewd and successful businessman. When he died in 1854, he left no will. For reasons unknown, Mollie inherited her father's estate, yet she relied on her half-brother James Woodroof for business advice, although it is believed that he received little or nothing upon his step-father's death.

Mollie did not suffer fools gladly. She was suspicious, and obsessively wiped her dinner plate repeatedly before eating food from it. A young man once proposed marriage to her, but the contentious Mollie dismissed him rudely as he pledged his love and devotion on bended knee.

Perhaps Mollie had reasons for her paranoia. She may have felt that everyone was trying to pry her loose from her wealth. Many years later, her obituary described her as equal to any man in business affairs, as if it were a trait only a man could have!

It was rumored that Mollie's half-brother, James Woodroof, borrowed money from Mollie either before or during the War Between the States. According to the rumor, James Woodroof attempted to repay the loan in Confederate money. It was totally useless at the end of the war! Mollie was still so angry at the time she made her will in 1876, she left him only $20.

Although Mollie was only 47 at the time she wrote her first will, she was in Nashville for surgery to remove a tumor from her breast. Fearing that she would not survive the surgery, she had a will hastily drawn up. Her fortune was left to various beneficiaries, including bequests to cousins in Georgia that she had never met, and a cousin who married into the Hundley family of Mooresville.

Her cousin Frances Hundley accompanied her to Nashville to comfort the ailing Mollie. But it was her unusual gift to future ministers of the Cumberland Presbyterian Church that would prompt accusations of theft, and keeps her name well known to this day.

By the time Mollie drew up her will, she had become a devoted supporter of the Cumberland Presbyterian Church. The brick church in Mooresville, a landmark in North Alabama, was built in the early 1800s as a joint effort of the residents. Although it was intended that a different denomination take over the church every year, Rev. Robert Donnell refused to vacate the pulpit at the culmination of his year, and after much dissension, he and the Cumberland Presbyterians occupied the church for many years.

Contrary to her personality, Mollie was generous to causes she believed in, usually giving more than was asked of her. Mollie donated the beautiful chandeliers in the brick church, one of which still remains. It was believed that she donated the steeple on the Athens Presbyterian Church as well.

The late William Pickens Drake detailed Mollie's friendship, as well as her many quirks, in his book "X + Y = Z or The Sleeping Preacher, Centennial Edition." The primary subject of the book was the Reverend Constantine Sanders, known all over as the "Sleeping Preacher" for the peculiar powers he exhibited after suffering a bout of typhoid fever at age 23.

Reverend Sanders's trances could come on at any time with no warning. He would appear to fall asleep, yet could carry on conversations and even speak and write in languages he had never studied. The personality of these trances was referred to as "X + Y = Z" by the personality itself. "X" could read unopened letters, describe events as they happened in other locations, and find lost items. Reverend Sanders suffered physically while in these trances, and one night he wished to hear a visiting minister give a sermon twelve miles away, but he was in the throes of one of his episodes, and too ill to attend. Amazingly, he wrote down the outline and highlights from his sick bed as it was given at the church, and it was later verified by the visiting minister himself!

Mollie Walton was a good friend of Reverend Sanders. She loaned her cottage for his family to live in while he was the minister in Mooresville. She also made her carriage and horse available to him. She spent a considerable amount of time with him, and had witnessed many of his clairvoyant episodes. Once, while riding through the woods, Reverend Sanders instructed the driver to stop. He stepped out of the carriage, and much to the surprise of the driver and Miss Walton, Reverend Sanders walked up to a wild fox in the woods and petted it. On another occasion, there was a gathering in Mooresville where non-believers made a list of questions that they felt sure he could not answer, and thus he would be revealed as a fraud. The person who volunteered to deliver the list of questions was surprised to find Reverend Sanders waiting for him with the list of answers, already written down.

Reverend Sanders despised the condition that made him famous. He asked his good friend Reverend G.W. Mitchell to write the original book about him, in order to clear up the many misconceptions and rumors about him. At first he felt that this phenomena was of the devil, but eventually he felt that it was a divine gift from God. Whatever it was, he would have rather been known as a good and humble minister than a freak. There were some who called him a fraud, but the many people who witnessed the unbelievable events that happened to him knew that there was no earthly explanation for the bizarre events that happened wherever he went. Reverend Sanders died on Good Friday, April 14, 1911.

Mollie Walton witnessed many of Reverend Sanders' supernatural episodes firsthand. As a close friend of his, he surely influenced her relationship with the church. Mollie generously remembered the Cumberland Presbyterians in her 1876 will. She left 600 of the original estate of 2,000 acres of farmland in the care of three trustees, who were instructed to lease the farm land, and give the proceeds to deserving young men who needed money to complete their religious education.

Mollie did not die as a result of her surgery in Nashville. She returned to Mooresville and, according to her half-brother's family, forgave him and welcomed him back into her good graces.

Faye Axford and Christine Edwards wrote another interesting story about Mollie in their book, "The Lure and Lore of Limestone County." Mollie had a cook named Aunt Tildy who lived, with her husband, in a small house in back of hers. One day, Aunt Tildy failed to show up for work, and was gone for three days before she returned with the excuse that she had gone to visit her sister. When asked where her husband was, she replied that she assumed he was at their home out back. Since no one had seen him since before Aunt Tildy left, they went to look for him. They found him, hacked to death with an ax. Aunt Tildy was arrested for her husband's murder, but because she was such an excellent cook, she spent her jail time in the kitchen.

Mollie lived another 23 years after her surgery. Her brother had already preceded her in death by the time she died on January 10, 1899. Major Woodroof's family went through her belongings and found her 1876 will, the one cutting them out of her fortune! They pleaded with the judge to understand that she had written a new will leaving everything to them, but he refused to let them have her estate until the new will could be produced. If in fact there was another will, it was never found. The irony is, that if the Woodroofs had not turned in the old will, they may have inherited everything.

The Woodroofs contested the will three times, taking it as high as the Alabama Supreme Court. Their lawsuits, recorded as Woodroof vs. Hundley, were based on claims that Mollie had discussed the new will among family members and disclosed that she had changed it in favor of the Woodroofs. They also argued that two of the three named beneficiaries had predeceased Mollie. As far as the trust for the Cumberland Presbyterians, the family pointed out that the name of the Presbytery was identified in her will as the Alabama Presbytery, though no such organization ever existed. At the time of the will, north Alabama fell under the jurisdiction of the Tennessee Presbytery, and at the time of her actual death, it had become the Robert Donnell Presbytery.

In the interpretation of the legalese, it was decided that the court, not the presbytery, would appoint the trustees to decide who would benefit from the trust. But for reasons that will never be known, the Cumberland Presbyterians failed to pursue the funds that she had intended for their use. One of the speculations is that, at the time of her death, there were internal struggles in the church over uniting with the Presbyterian U.S.A. denomination. Possibly, the pro-union members did not feel any moral obligation to let the anti-union members know about the trust. Also, the one surviving trustee was a devout member of the Church of Christ.

When the one trustee died in 1920, a sole trustee was appointed. What happened with the proceeds of the farm for the next 55 years, is only a guess, but the word embezzlement has been suggested by some. It wasn't until 1975 that William Pickens Drake stumbled on the situation by accident, and led the effort which finally carried out Mollie Walton's wishes.

Meanwhile, in the many years in which unnamed individuals received the benefits of the trust, the Tennessee Valley Authority condemned 150 acres of Mollie's plantation for TVA use. Mollie had also specified that the four acres in her property that contained the family cemetery be maintained in perpetuity. It was discovered that, because of the fine fence surrounding the cemetery, it was being used as a hog pen.

With the permission of the court, the land was auctioned in 1991, and the interest is now used to educate young ministers. Over $75,000 is given annually under the supervision of three trustees, members of the Cumberland

Presbyterian Church.   Mollie's wishes are finally being carried out.

Approximately one month before Mollie's death, she moved into the home of Mary Hays, who, in a deposition, said that Mollie was a considerable nuisance to the household.   Although Mollie paid the family for their services during her final illness, Mrs. Hays filed a claim against the estate for an additional $500 for looking after Mollie, and having to put up with her disagreeable attitude. The judge awarded her $150 plus interest.

So many mysteries revolve around Mollie Walton today.   Her will has disappeared from the file in the Limestone County Courthouse in Athens.   The final unanswered question is the location of her grave. Although she owned several plots in Maple Hill Cemetery in Huntsville, and although her own immediate family is buried in the family cemetery near Mooresville, it is believed that she is not buried in any of the plots she owned. Her obituary tells us that she was interred at Maple Hill, but there is no marker over her grave. Ironically, the Hundleys and Woodroofs, who faced each other in court on three occasions, face each other in death, separated by a narrow road in Maple Hill. Could she be buried in one of those plots? No one will ever know.

For Mollie Walton, who left so many lasting legacies, it is a shame that her money could not buy a lasting monument to her.

John Haywood Jones's home

From a Kingdom in Wales to a Cotton Farm in Alabama

Llywelyn ap Gruffudd was the last Welsh-born ruler of his country. As the Prince of Wales, he was killed while fighting against the army of England's King Edward I, the brutal "Hammer of the Scots." Llywelyn's severed head was displayed at the Tower of London on a spiked gate as a grisly warning to other potential traitors.

Three decades earlier, the Treaty of Montgomery was signed in 1267 by England's King Henry III. Essentially, it would allow the Welsh people to be ruled by one of their own countrymen. Just five years later, King Edward I set out to conquer Scotland and Wales to establish a unified British continent. His battles against William Wallace, Robert the Bruce, and their fellow Scots in the ensuing years are well known to many, but his annihilation of the Welsh was just as bloody. His thirst for complete domination would earn King Edward I the everlasting hatred of their descendants for centuries to come.

According to one source, Lylwelyn was imprisoned at the Tower of London. *Officially,* he fell to his death while trying to escape from a high window and his hastily - made rope broke. *Unofficially,* the rope was tossed out the window after he fell to his death.

When King Edward's son, Edward II, was born at the Welsh castle at Caernarfon in 1300, the king added insult to injury by giving his infant the title, Lord Edward, Prince of Wales. With the exception of Edward II's own son, the tradition of naming the first-born male of the ruling monarch of England, "Prince of Wales," continues to this day.

Among the descendants of Llywelyn ap Gruffudd was Reverend Rowland Jones. Born in Swinbrook Oxfordshire in 1608, he was the vicar of St. James Church at Dorney, Buckinghamshire, England from 1667 - 1685. Today, his name appears on a framed roll inside the small church, which dates back to the 12th century. The historic Dorney Parish Church looks much like it did in Rev. Jones's time.

His son, Rowland Jones, Jr., a vicar at Little Kimble, Buckinghamshire England, came to America in about 1674. He became the first vicar of Bruton Parish, the brick church

at Williamsburg, Virginia. Rev. Rowland Jones preached
the dedicatory sermon of the new brick church on January
6, 1684, the day of Epiphany. According to *Historical
Southern Families*, the salary of the minister was set at 1,600
pounds of tobacco and cask per year. The cost of interment
inside the church was established at 500 pounds of tobacco.
For burial in the chancel area, the cost was 1,000 pounds of
tobacco. Digging a grave would cost the survivors 10
pounds of tobacco. The baptismal font, imported in 1691, is
believed to be the same one that is today placed over the
headstone of Rev. Rowland Jones, Jr.

His headstone, in addition to those of his son Orlando
and daughter-in-law Martha, are incorporated into the floor
in the chancel area of Bruton Parish. The Williamsburg
home of Orlando Jones is one of the many interesting
restoration projects of recent years.

Orlando Jones's granddaughter became a famous
person in America's history - Martha Washington. Another
granddaughter would marry Captain John Jones of the 6th
Virginia Regiment. He and his son Llewellen Jones (records
indicate many variations of the spelling of his name) spent
the miserable winter of 1778 at Valley Forge with cousin
Martha's husband, George.

On June 13, 1776, Llewellen Jones received a commission signed by John Hancock, president of the Continental Congress. In addition to having fought at Brandywine, Germantown, and Trenton, New Jersey, Captain Jones was with General Washington when they crossed the Delaware.

Llewellen Jones came to north Alabama at about the same time as a group of influential and politically aggressive people from Petersburg, Georgia. Jones was part of the "Georgia Faction," although he apparently had no political aspirations for himself. He purchased 640 acres at the 1809 land sale south of Huntsville's Big Spring and by 1811, he owned over 1,000 acres in the county. In addition, he also owned lots 41 and 42 on Fountain Row and acquired property from a debt owed to him by Irby Jones. He named that plantation Avalon, and today much of the property is occupied by the University of Alabama in Huntsville. He also bought property in and around the community of Greenbrier in Limestone County, known as Druid's Grove. For his daughter, Maria Perkins, he bought land in Lawrence County, appropriately named Seclusion.

Surprisingly, the name Llewellen Jones was common among men of Welsh ancestry. Three men by that name settled in north Alabama, and their records continue to be

222

mistakenly intertwined with each other. In January 1829, one of these men was hanged for murdering his brother-in-law, while another died of natural causes in 1828. But the Llewellen Jones who had been a soldier in the Revolutionary War, would die much more mysteriously.

Llewellen Jones seemed to be on top of the world. His fortune in cotton was increased in 1818 when cotton sold for twenty-five cents per pound. Then in 1819, cotton prices spiraled downward and the extreme financial straits that first hit the cotton farmer rippled to everyone who depended on cotton in one way or another. The financial panic of 1819 hit Jones hard, and nearing the age of 60, he felt he could not cope.

In a letter dated January 27, 1820 to Senator John Williams Walker, also a member of the Georgia Faction, a friend wrote, "Llewellen Jones put a period to his existence last night by hanging himself,..."

On Saturday, January 29, 1820, the *Alabama Republican* ran the following story:

"Suicide - On Wednesday the 26th instant Mr. Lewelling Jones, resident in the vicinity of this place, put an end to his existence, by hanging himself with his pocket handkerchief. Mr. Jones was a man in affluent circumstances, and had just moved to a beautiful country seat near Huntsville, which he had recently

*purchased.   No probable cause has been assigned, for his
committing this violence on himself."*   According to local
gossip, he hanged himself from a joist in the home that was
still under construction.

Jones's survivors would weather the cotton crisis, as
did   countless   others   who   were   affected   even   more
seriously. Llewellen's son Alexander inherited Avalon, and
his other son, John Nelson Spotswood Jones, who was an
attorney in Huntsville, lived at Druid's Grove with his large
family. His law office doubled as the first public library in
the state of Alabama.

Family records for the next forty-five years indicate
prosperity and prominence for the Jones descendants. The
Civil War brought another kind of crisis that would
financially destroy them. Their homes and fortunes were
decimated.   John Nelson Spotswood Jones and his wife
were already deceased before the war, along with several of
their children. Their son, John Haywood Jones, had just
completed his beautiful home on Clinton Street in Athens,
Alabama when Col. Turchin and his men came to call
during the infamous Sack of Athens. The devastation of his
home and his life were apparently too much for him to
bear.   According   to   a   family   story,   John   went   to
Chattanooga where he checked into an inn and drank

himself into a coma that resulted in his death. His 10-year-old son died 5 days later. Their graves are in the Jones-Donnell cemetery in a Greenbrier cotton field. Headstones there mirror the ebb and flow of family fortune. Before the war, elaborate works of art grace the graves of those privileged people who lived at Druid's Grove, while just a few short years later, sunken earth is all that remains of the now-anonymous people who died prematurely.

Today, there are still unanswered questions. Alexander Jones, who inherited Avalon, never married, but had children by a slave. He was described as a "peculiar old botchler." It was said that he would buy old horses, knowing they would be of no use to him on his plantation. To his credit, he treated them humanely until their deaths.

Alexander's descendants continued to live at Avalon until the land was appropriated for the college campus in Huntsville. They remain proud of their heritage and have become scholars of the Jones family and its contribution to North Alabama.

After his suicide, Llewellen Jones was buried in an unmarked grave in a Jones family cemetery that is behind present-day Morton Hall on the UAH campus. In the 1970s, the Twickenham Town Chapter, Daughters of the American Revolution, marked his grave in a beautiful public ceremony. While many of the Jones descendants wondered why such a wealthy man's grave was left unmarked for so long, it only recently became clear that the details of his death were carefully excised from the family records. Perhaps his immediate family felt the stigma of his suicide and chose not to erect a marker.

For whatever reason he chose to hang himself, there is evidence that some anonymous person does not condemn his action. Visitors who occasionally wander to the small cemetery surrounded by a wrought-iron fence, find that he is appropriately honored for his contribution to American freedom. Each year around Memorial Day, a small American flag is placed on the grave of patriot Llewellen Jones.

Sweet Home Alabama

Lucy Judkins looked up at the picture on the wall and wished with all her might that she could go back home. The little girl in the picture looked cold as she skipped happily through snow wearing her coat and bonnet. Lucy didn't care that she was surrounded by exotic flowers and birds at her home in South America. She wanted to go back to Alabama!

Lucy was born in Tuskegee, Alabama in January, 1865. Her father recorded her birth in the family Bible: "...as her star rose upon the horizon of the world, the star of the government of the Confederate States sank to rest forever."

When the Civil War ended three months later, the southern countryside was charred and devastated. Whether the citizens of the South were rich or poor before the war, they were now alike in destitution. Southerners were left homeless, penniless, and without hope. Some families packed up what was left and went to Texas to start over. Land was cheap and the sentiment of Texans was the same as their own. Most importantly, the northern carpetbaggers weren't interested in punishing the Texans. "Gone to Texas" was scrawled on the doorways of abandoned homes.

Still others embarked on a more uncertain future in an effort to recapture the essence of the Old South. Emperor Dom Pedro II offered the best deal to Southern Americans to entice them to Brazil, the only country where owning slaves was legal, though importing slaves was illegal. Slavery was not what brought Confederates to Brazil, it was the absence of Yankees! Southerners could buy land for 22 cents per acre and they were met with fanfare. High quality cotton could be planted once every five years and two crops per year could be harvested. Of the 154 families that have been positively identified as immigrants, 37 were from Alabama and 103 were from Texas, though many of those Texans were transplants from other southern states.

John Judkins left his 7,000 acre Tuskegee, Alabama plantation known as The Bluff, along with several members of his family. The Bluff had been a society in itself. He employed a full-time physician, cabinet-maker, and two teachers for the schoolhouse built for the plantation children.

When John Judkins' son left home to fight for the Confederacy, Judkins knew he may never see his son again.

Those fears were realized when word came that his son was killed. John's greatest sorrow was that his son's body was never recovered and brought home for burial.

John had been elected to the Alabama Legislature from Macon County in 1866. He resigned to leave Alabama with three generations of the Judkins family to move to a country where they didn't understand a word of the Portuguese language. On February 27, 1867, Alabama Governor Robert Patton signed a heartfelt letter of recommendation for John C. Judkins. He finished it by saying, "We commend him most heartily to the kind attention of all to whom these presents may come, and the best wish that we can give him is that he may find friends in his new home with hearts as kind and as true as his own." It was also signed by a Chief Justice, Associate Justice, Attorney General, three judges, and ex-Governor J. H. Watts. Clearly, John Judkins was a very prominent Alabama citizen!

His granddaughter Lucy described their new life in Brazil through the pure eyes of an innocent child. Her grandfather made the first exploratory trip to Brazil, after traveling to New York with his two sons, and Colonels Shackelford and Watson, where they would board a steamer to Brazil. Although he vowed not to speak to any Yankees unless absolutely necessary, they found that the only two hotels in New York where a respectable Southerner would lodge, were full. Lucy wrote, "…in their present dilemma they were forced to make inquiries, and so [John Judkins] began addressing any chance passerby with the introductory remark 'that they were strangers in the city and on their way to *Brazeel* and would like to be directed to a hotel.' My uncles said it was certainly unnecessary to make the statement that they were strangers as the fact was ridiculously obvious."

One of the shiploads of Confederados, or Confederates, arrived in April 1866 after a harrowing journey that nearly landed them in Africa. Apparently, the ladies stored their metal skirt hoops underneath the ship's compass, causing false readings and sending the ship in the wrong direction.

In 1867, plans were finalized and at last the Judkins family was en route to Brazil. Lucy was tired of the long ocean voyage, and when her father excitedly exclaimed, "Yonder's land!" Lucy ran to her mother asking for a shawl to put over her head. She explained to her mother that the little girls in the picture books were always dressed this way when they got off their ships.

The Judkins settled on a 30,000 acre plantation named Fazenda du Bangu in the Corcovado Mountain Range. It had been the home of Baron de Pera, the Minister of

Agriculture under Dom Pedro II. Lucy's grandfather paid $30,000 in gold for the plantation, the enormous house, and the exquisite furnishings. The Judkins house became a popular vacation spot for the many family members left in the United States. Lucy learned the Negro-Portuguese dialect from the slaves at Fazenda du Bangu and the children of the slaves became her playmates. But she still looked at the picture of the little girl in the snow and longed to come back to Alabama.

The Judkins family enjoyed the company of many other Confederados, including the descendants of Revolutionary War Soldier John Wade Keyes from Athens, Alabama. John Keyes came to Brazil with the Gunter Colony and became the personal dentist for Emperor Dom Pedro, who treated the colonists as if they were royalty.

The beautiful flowers and fruits of Brazil were like none the Americans had ever seen. Rare birds, butterflies, and monkeys were a constant source of curiosity. In spite of all this, the Americans became homesick. Classic literature had to be sent from friends in Alabama. Even worse, farmers failed because they weren't familiar with the complications found in farming the strange soil and climate conditions. The language proved to be an even larger barrier and Lucy's grandfather could never learn

Portuguese well enough to give concise directions to the slaves. He knew that certain words were reversed in the Portuguese language, so after realizing that the servants in the field did not understand "turn around," he would yell, "around turn" - in English. They still didn't understand. Finally, Dom Pedro, after luring the Americans with promises of recreating their old lifestyles, wanted the slaves freed.

After three years in Brazil, the Judkins returned to Alabama. They and their slaves cried as they said good-bye, and the slaves begged to come with them. Some of the Confederados remained in Brazil, hoping to someday return home to die and be buried in Southern soil. They never did. A separate cemetery was established for the Americans who were denied burial in the Catholic cemeteries. Their descendants married Brazilians, but carefully taught their Southern customs and dialect to their children.

The dialect found in the Southern United States today bears the influence of our contact with non-southerners and no longer resembles that of our ancestors. To hear the accent spoken by our ancestors before the Civil War, you would have to travel much farther south - to the South

American colonies in Brazil known as Americana, Santa Barbara, and Campo.

John Judkins died in 1871 and was buried on the Tallapoosa River. Lucy's father, James, became the County Solicitor of Elmore County when he returned. He then became the Inspector of Penitentiary, Assistant U.S. Attorney for the middle district of Alabama, and then practiced law in Wetumpka. Lucy married John Durr, a wholesale grocer and druggist. She recalled only fond memories of her brief time in Brazil.

The descendants of John Judkins left lasting legacies to the state of Alabama. Harry Pennington graduated from Wetumpka High School and after serving in the Army in World War II, he became a lawyer, circuit solicitor, circuit judge, State Representative, Executive Secretary to Governor George Wallace, and president of Huntsville Lumber Company. Lucy Judkins Durr's picture of the little girl in the snowstorm now hangs in the Huntsville home of Harry and Gloria Pennington.

Today, the descendants of the Confederados still gather to sing "Dixie" and other Southern anthems in memory of their Confederate ancestors. Amidst the headstones of Southern families, they spread blankets and eat fried chicken while speaking Southern English and wearing ante-

233

bellum clothing. Thanks to the descendants of the Confederate exiles, the historic Southern dialect and old-time customs will never die.

Warriors In the Pacific

Hitler's bloody reign brought terror and misery to millions of Europeans in the course of World War II. By 1941, Great Britain and Russia continued to give their all, but they began to lose ground, having already lost France to the German Army. In the Far East, Japan had invaded China and Southeast Asia. The United States put pressure on Japan to withdraw its forces from occupied territories with an oil embargo. In the summer of 1941, Japanese and American diplomats met in Washington, D.C. for negotiations. In spite of these efforts, the Japanese were already putting the finishing touches on their plans to attack Pearl Harbor.

With the world about to be engulfed in war, communications between countries were frantic and clarity was critical. But within governments and within armies, secret communications were difficult, and encoding these messages a matter of survival. We have heard the stories about the code breakers, but what of the code makers?

This is a story about the efforts of a few men whose contribution toward the war effort saved thousands of American lives. One man's unusual suggestion appeared too simple, too good to be true, but his incredible idea created the now legendary Navajo CodeTalker.

The Navajo Indians are thought to be descendants of ancient Chinese Mongolians. Physical characteristics tend to support this claim. It is surmised that tribes of Mongolians migrated across a land bridge known now as the Bering Strait, and settled for a time in present-day Alaska. There are many language similarities between some Alaskan Eskimos and Navajos, as well as Athabascan-speaking tribes in Canada.

The reasons the Mongolians left China can only be assumed. Perhaps they were forced out as a result of war, or a search for water, food, or just better living conditions. With the gradual melting of the Ice Age glaciers, it became possible for the wandering tribes to come southward. At the same time the Bering Strait became covered with water as the ice melted, making it impossible for the migrators to return to China.

The Navajos eventually settled in the American Southwest, along with other Indian tribes. These tribes did not co-exist peacefully, but they eventually banded together with the arrival of the Spanish Conquistadors, their common enemy.

Philip Johnston, a civil engineer from Los Angeles, was the son of a missionary sent to live and work with the Navajos at around the turn of the century. As a young boy, he became fluent in the Navajo language, an unwritten language taught orally from one generation to the next. In 1942, Johnston, who was a veteran of WW I, requested special permission to enlist in the Marine Corps with a noncommissioned rank. Johnston was in his forties at the time, and feeling that time was of the essence, he did not seek a commission for fear that he would not only be rejected, but the response would take too long.

Johnston proposed that the U.S. Marine Corps use specially trained Navajos in combat to send crucial messages across battlefields. Choctaws and Comanches had served in similar capacities in WW I. This was over 20 years later however, and technology had progressed to the point that Americans were constantly developing new codes as enemy interception plagued the safety and secrecy of our operations. Johnston was certain that the unwritten Navajo language could not be understood by the Japanese, who up to that time had successfully decoded combat messages. English-speaking Anglos find the dialect nearly impossible to understand, much less speak.

Although the Navajo language did not include many of the terms commonly used in warfare, certain Navajo words could easily be adapted, thus confusing the Japanese even further. The end result was actually a code within the Navajo language; therefore, Navajos who were not code talkers, but were fluent in the language, could not even break the code themselves.

The idea was met with some hesitation. Navajos, on the whole, had good reasons to distrust the white man, or Anglos as they are known. Government officials had given their word and gone back on it too many times. Indians recalled their forefathers' stories about their imprisonment at the hands of the U.S. Army in the late 1800's, for fighting to save their lands.

The Navajo culture was completely foreign to Anglo Americans. The concept of owning land was unheard of to the Navajos; they simply borrowed the land for their necessities, such as grazing animals. They lived in dwellings called hogans, built with the door always facing the Talking God, who dwelled in the East.

Navajos did not share the Anglo preoccupation with time. They did not engage in small talk and spoke only when necessary, and then quite briefly. This manner was misinterpreted by Anglos as being unfriendly or even rude.

The ancient communication of warriors was developed by many tribes of Indians back when they were at war with each other. The Plains Indians delivered crucial information using message sticks. Notches were carved on these sticks detailing necessary information, that if intercepted by an enemy tribe, could not be deciphered.

When Japan attacked Pearl Harbor, Americans were outraged, fearing that the west coast of the United States would be the next Japanese target. The Navajos of the Southwest shared this fear, and when the call came to enlist, Indians proudly stood in line. Their desire to fight however, had nothing to do with fighting for the ideals of the white man. Since 1938, they had also followed the events of the war carefully, and their reason for enlisting was simple - to protect Mother Earth. Immediately after the Pearl Harbor bombing was announced, young Navajos began packing up their hunting rifles and belongings, some tied in simple bandannas. The Tribal Council had already issued a resolution affirming that hostile acts against the U.S. Government would be considered hostile to Navajos as well.

In April, 1942, Marine Corps recruiters came to the reservations ready to implement Johnston's plan to train code talkers. Some Navajos were clearly underage, but their dates of birth could not be exactly pinpointed because the Navajos kept no written birth records. Those not completely fluent in both English and Navajo were not selected, and even some Anglos, who had traded with the Navajos, tried to enlist as code talkers. Unfortunately, their knowledge of the language consisted of terms specific to buying and selling, known as "trading-post Navajo."

The recruits were chosen, and for many, ceremonial rituals were performed before their departure. These three day ceremonies imparted protection upon the young warriors. Some carried special feathers, medicine pouches, or other talismans with them as they went to war. Family members had special ceremonies throughout the war asking for the spiritual protection and guidance of their soldiers so far from home.

As a Marine Corps Staff Sergeant, Johnston's job was to recruit and train the code talkers, as well as implement his plan. Of his initial request for 200 Navajos, Washington gave permission to recruit only 30 for a pilot project. Of that first group sent to San Diego for basic training, only one did not complete the rigorous training. For many of them, this was their first time away from home, first time on a train, first time in a motel. The Navajo tradition of sleeping when tired, and eating when hungry was replaced with drill instructors dictating - loudly - their every movement.

The first 29 recruits actually developed the code, and they were able to relay and decipher with amazing accuracy and speed. They developed new words for the many military terms which had no Navajo counterpart. The Navajo word for chicken hawk referred to a dive bomber, staring owl was an observation plane, buzzard became bomber. Using these guttural, tongue-twisting sounds, they added some amusing terms to their war vocabulary. "Rolled hat" was the word for Australia, "braided hair" was the term for China, "bounded by water" became the term for Britain. Their final test was a competition against the standard equipment of that time. The machine took four hours to relay and decode a message. The Navajos took 2 1/2 minutes. They were ready for battle.

Marines were shipped to notorious islands such as Okinawa, Iwo Jima, Guadalcanal, the Marshall Islands, and Saipan. The horrors of war would visit them first-hand. Japanese soldiers hid in the craggy roots of Joshua trees, buried themselves in sand and volcanic ash, and set booby traps to sabotage the Marines coming in via amphibious landings. The Japanese had vowed to fight to the death, as it was considered a dishonor against their nation to surrender or be captured alive.

The code talkers were not among the first wave of Marines to land; their survival was considered crucial to saving other lives. Of course it was necessary to have them perform other regular duties when not stationed at the radio. Upon hearing the code words, "Arizona" and "New Mexico," they were immediately summoned to send or receive a coded message.

The Navajos had a fear of death, believing that the evil from the dead person would return to seek revenge. The stillness of the pre-dawn was the most terrifying time for all of these young Americans, regardless of color. The knowledge that the coming day may be their last on this earth filled them with fear and anxiety. Many of the code talkers began each day with a ritual of placing corn pollen on their tongues to ensure clear and accurate message relays.

These young Indians left the harsh, but peaceful beauty of mesas and arroyos to find themselves crouched in damp foxholes with descendants of their ancestral enemies, united in their cause to fight a new enemy. The Japanese physically favored the Navajos much more than the Anglo Americans. For this reason, many Navajos found themselves looking down the length of a bayonet at an American who had mistaken them for a Japanese soldier. To Americans, the gibberish of the Japanese language sounded close enough to Navajo, and some Japanese had learned English well enough to send false messages to the Americans over the radio. The answer to this curious phenomena became clear as Marines came across the occasional dead body of a Japanese soldier wearing a class ring from an American university.

After a few of these mistaken identity mishaps, an Anglo soldier was assigned to every code talker. The code talkers were given two code numbers. If they were captured by the Japanese, who were now well aware of the Navajo talkers, and forced to send a message, they were to use one code number to inform Americans of their capture. On one occasion, a Navajo was captured and tortured to reveal the code. Because he was not trained as a code talker, the code made no sense to him, and he nearly lost his life over it.

The Navajos were no different than other Americans when it came to bravery in battle. Some especially courageous Navajos would strip down to the waist and walk across enemy lines to mingle with the Japanese who mistook them for their own soldiers. One Navajo actually strolled into at least two Japanese "nests" with a submachine gun and killed everyone inside; sadly, he was later killed in battle. One Navajo was known to scalp Japanese soldiers he had killed.

By now the Japanese were also aware of the ease of which Navajos were mistaken for their own soldiers. The Japanese instituted a system where they would tap each other on the leg twice, expecting the same signal in return. One intuitive Navajo watched in hiding until he was able to figure out the code, then went in himself to infiltrate the enemy for valuable information.

Skills developed and honed by their ancient ancestors served them well in battle. Using all of their senses, they detected danger and crawled silently at night much better than other Marines.

After the initial success of the Navajos, the recruitment goal was increased to 25 per month. The Navajo tribe was the largest in the United States, but their illiteracy rate was also the highest. The advantage of using Navajos in particular, was that before the war, German students had studied with other Indian tribes, and could presumably understand a code that would have been developed by, for example, the Choctaws. There were only 28 non-Navajo Americans who had any knowledge of the language.

As the war progressed, new weapons and military terms were added to the English language. It was necessary to develop new Navajo counterparts as well, and it was decided that the code talkers should all meet on occasion to sharpen their skills and learn new words.

On one training exercise held in the Hawaiian Islands, the Marines were sent into the desert on a two-day march with only one canteen of water. By the beginning of the second day, the non-Navajo Marines had given out completely for lack of water. The Navajos, having extracted the liquid from prickly pear cactus leaves, still had plenty of water in their canteens and were ready to roll.

These men were able to quickly and successfully report enemy movement, saving untold American lives. There were times when the Americans found themselves under fire from other Americans as they moved positions. Code talkers communicating to each other from different units were able to avoid deadly "friendly fire."

Navajo code talkers were among the shiploads of Marines enroute to Japan when news that the atomic bomb had been dropped was announced. Those who went on to land in Japan witnessed the burned and flattened rubble where cities once stood. They described sleeping huts made by Japanese who had lost their homes. These huts were eerily similar to their huts back home on the reservation.

With the end of years of hard fighting, young Americans turned their thoughts towards returning home and rebuilding their lives. For the Navajos, it was an especially tough adjustment. Some felt that they could not possibly return to the reservation after what they had witnessed and lived through. A few married women outside their culture, and remained in foreign countries. Some simply left the service and were never heard from again. Others came home wondering how their skills with the radio could be used on a reservation that was still not equipped with electricity.

These WWII warriors returned home and went through the tribal ceremony known as the Enemy Way. They removed their military uniform and other trappings of the war, then walked into their homes for a spiritual cleansing and removal of evil.

Fortunately, as they looked around at the old life and the nearly 40 percent unemployment rate, many took advantage of the GI Bill to get a college education. They were ready to make a difference for themselves and their people. Some became well known educators, artists, and officials at the Bureau of Indian Affairs. A site was established in Los Angeles for many Navajos who went there in search of a different way of life. The center was a place they could come to for sanctuary from a world that didn't always understand or embrace them.

Sadly, the incredible impact of the code talkers was not recognized for many years because the operation itself was still classified. Although they had the respect of their fellow Marines, who in some cases owed their very lives to these code talkers, national recognition was still forthcoming. Unofficial estimates place the number of code talkers between 375 and 420, an astonishingly small number of men whose service saved thousands of Americans.

A former code talker from New Mexico explained their reluctance to talk about the war after their return. He explained that there is a tendency to glamorize war after the fact. Movies and books glorify the aggression and bloodshed that should be kept in a proper perspective, especially for impressionable young people. There is an ancient Indian belief that experiences are learned through contact with one's five senses. When children see the violence of war on television or in a movie, they are using only the senses of sight and sound. Without the sense of smell, one cannot experience the acrid scent of gunpowder or the sickening stench of burning flesh. Without the sense of touch, one cannot feel the pain of injury, or the discomfort of cold, heat, or wet. The movie experience does not offer the taste of mud, gunpowder, or hunger.

In 1989, a statue of a young Indian was unveiled in the Phoenix Plaza in Arizona. The seated Indian bore the high cheekbones and wore a turquoise necklace characteristic of the Navajo. In his right hand, he holds the flute, signaling the end of confrontation and coming of peace. It is a beautiful commemoration to the brave warriors known as the Navajo Code Talkers.

Attack at Dawn

When Luther Tidwell said good-bye to his family, they all knew too well the possibility that they might never see him again. He was required to make the ultimate sacrifice for his country if he had to, but on March 19, 1945, Seaman First Class Luther Tidwell cheated death twice - on the same morning!

Luther Tidwell, a tall, handsome young man with blue eyes and dark hair, had just completed his junior year at Madison County High School in Gurley, Alabama. Luther was always different from the rest of the boys his age, somehow more mature and responsible. Early on cold mornings, he would go to the elementary school in Big Cove and start the fire to get the school building warm for the young students. Then he would catch the bus over to Gurley, where he attended school.

Big Cove, Alabama was a small community in a fertile valley at the foot of the Appalachian Mountain chain. Although it was just over Monte Sano Mountain from the larger town of Huntsville, Big Cove seemed unaffected and isolated from Huntsville. Around the Tidwell home were acres of corn, beans, and cotton.

Luther was the youngest child in a large farm family, and his mother had died when he was 16. His five surviving older brothers and sisters watched over him protectively. Luther turned 18 on May 12, 1944, and only a few days later, he received his draft notice. His family went into shock, and for the next month, they all lived in a fog of gloom and worry.

When Luther arrived at Ft. McClellan for processing, he was asked, "What branch of the service would you prefer?"

Luther couldn't swim, so he knew he didn't want to go to the Navy. He asked to be sent to the Marines or the Army.

"You'll make a good sailor." It was already going badly for him.

On the bus to Birmingham, he had yet another chance to avoid the Navy. A Marine recruiter boarded the bus and asked for five volunteers to become Marines. Six men, including Luther, volunteered. The recruiter settled it by handing out six straws, and whoever chose the short straw would continue on to the Navy. Luther Tidwell got the short straw.

Luther arrived at Great Lakes for a 90-day training period. The sailors were issued dog tags, but they had to purchase their own chain for them. Luther walked into a small establishment and said to the woman behind the counter, "I need a chain to put my dog tags on."

"Say again?" she asked.

"I need a chain to put my dog tags on."

"Repeat that please?" she asked again.

The obnoxious woman had gotten on his last nerve, and after asking him to repeat his statement for the fourth time, he angrily snapped, "I want a damn chain for my dog tags!"

The woman laughed as she explained to Luther that she was from Fayetteville, Tennessee, and just wanted to hear his Southern accent, a reminder of her home so far away.

Luther's training at Great Lakes was extended by two weeks, due to the company commander's nervous breakdown. The commander's replacement nearly died from a ruptured appendix.

Luther fared only slightly better. His swimming instructor informed Luther that he had the distinction of being the only person he could not teach to swim.

Still, the Navy didn't give up on him. After training, he came home for seven days, then he was sent by train to Shoemaker, California. His first Christmas away from home was spent on the train, and Christmas dinner consisted of a slice of bread, a baked potato, and a glass of water.

The *Franklin*, a 27,100 ton Essex class aircraft carrier, was commissioned in January, 1944. On October 13, 1944, a Japanese kamikaze plane crashed into the deck, skidded across, and into the water. Just a few days later on October 30, three kamikazes relentlessly pursued the *Franklin*. One narrowly missed the starboard side, one hit the flight deck, and the third missed, but crashed into the flight deck of the nearby *Belleau Wood*. The *Franklin* was hastily repaired at Puget Sound Naval Yard, and Luther Tidwell was aboard when it shipped out of Bremerton, Washington on February 2, 1945. The fifth fleet was headed toward Japan.

Luther, nicknamed "Buck" by his crew mates, missed his friends and family. He thought about the other boys he had grown up with, now playing high school basketball and baseball without him. On the ship, they were served fish every day at noon and evening meals, and he never liked it. He even quit trying to like it. He missed eating hamburgers, and one of the staples of the South, iced tea.

One of the many duties Luther found to be utterly useless, was that they were instructed to paint the gun turrets one day, wash them with diesel fuel the next day, shine them the day after, chip the paint off with a hammer and chisel the day after that, and then repeat the process. He realized that the intention was to keep them from getting bored, but to do something that didn't need to be done, seemed like a complete waste of time.

The fifth fleet controlled the waters 50 miles from the Japanese mainland, nearest the town of Kobe. Dive bombers and torpedo planes conducted successful strike attacks from the their homebase on the *Franklin*, sinking numerous ships, shooting down enemy aircraft, and destroying factories and warehouses as well. For six weeks, Luther watched Japanese bombers dot the sky. The crew of the *Franklin* was on alert at all times, with a crew stationed at the guns 24 hours a day.

On March 19, 1945, a Japanese bomber came out of the blinding sun headed straight for the *Franklin*. The Japanese pilot dropped two armor-piercing bombs. The first hit centerline on the flight deck, causing fires on the second and third decks. The second bomb hit aft and tore through two decks. Unfortunately, the American planes on the flight deck were loaded with fuel and armed bombs. The Japanese bombs set off multiple explosions and the ship and crew were in danger of becoming incinerated in a giant inferno. Thick black smoke rose up in ugly clouds, choking them and stinging their eyes. Men were dead everywhere, many blown off the ship, and the fire was quickly spreading.

With his mission accomplished, the Japanese pilot turned back toward Japan. He "hedge-hopped" through the many ships in the fleet, but was sent down in flames by combat air patrol.

Luther Tidwell had been on duty throughout the night of March 18-19. He had finished breakfast and had stepped in to his quarters just after dawn on March 19, when he felt the great ship shudder.

"This is it," he thought. He hoped it wasn't another kamikaze.

He reached for his 20mm rifle, but it was gone. Stepping back into the hallway, he met up with a Marine. Together, they went through the labyrinth of hallways, trying to find their way to a deck. They thought the ship was hit at or near the bow, and they wanted to get to the fan tail before the mighty ship turned into a sinking tomb.

Just a few seconds after the first bomb hit the ship, they felt another jolt from a second bomb.

Luther and the Marine got to the fan tail, but they were eerily alone. There was no damage where they were, but the fire was quickly spreading in their direction. Within a few seconds, a chief ran up and instructed them to start throwing ammunition overboard to keep it from exploding in the intense heat.

Suddenly, the Marine went wild with panic and tried to jump overboard. He was terrified of fire and had to be restrained by Luther and the chief until he could calm down. Luther, who habitually wore a life vest *and* a life belt because he could not swim, removed his life belt and secured it around the Marine. The Marine then started climbing a rope up onto the higher deck to escape the rushing fire. As he held on to the rope suspended between the two decks, the rope burned in two, and he plummeted into the cold Pacific waters. In his state of panic, he failed to inflate the belt. The young Marine perished in the waves.

With no time to think, Luther and the chief continued to throw crates of ammunition overboard. They wore asbestos gloves because the crates were dangerously hot from the fire all around them. Luther grabbed the last crate and heaved it overboard. He took one step back and watched in horror as the crate exploded, just a moment after he released his grip.

The mighty ship was listing on the starboard side. Fire was all around them, debris from the exploding bombs, shells, rockets, and planes rained down everywhere.

Luther and the chief saw only one option for them. They jumped into the water.

The chief took Luther's handkerchief and his own. Holding them together in one hand, he waved his arm in the air to get the attention of one of the smaller ships trying frantically to save the helpless crew members. Within about 200 feet from the burning *Franklin*, they were pulled aboard another ship.

The two men felt lucky to be alive as they stood on the deck to let the sun dry them off. Less than an hour later, Luther peered down into the water.

"Lookie yonder, Chief, there's a Japanese torpedo coming right at us."

For the second time that morning, Luther and the chief jumped into the frigid water. The torpedo was right on target; it scored a direct hit.

The two men were picked up by the British Coast Guard, and they remained on the ship throughout the night.

Surprisingly, the *Franklin* did not sink, although 724 brave men lost their lives that day, and another 265 were wounded. Another 710 men remained on the ship and prevented more damage. Amazingly, the ship was pulled toward Pearl Harbor for repairs, but soon she was traveling at 14 knots and continued on her own power. Those who saw the ship couldn't believe their eyes, the *Franklin* was now a blackened, burned-out hull.

Luther went aboard the *Franklin* one more time to retrieve his personal belongings. There was nothing left. With the exception of one man, everyone, including Luther, who jumped overboard without waiting for the command to abandon ship, was forbidden by the captain to serve again as a crewmember of the *Franklin*. The one exception was the 56-year-old chief that Luther had escaped death with, twice in one day.

Luther's next assignment was at the naval air station in Maui. It was a training base for pilots, and he was practically delirious to be to back on dry land. On August 6, one of the pilots told Luther that America had dropped the atomic bomb on Hiroshima. Nagasaki was bombed on August 9, and Japan surrendered. The men at the air station celebrated by jacking up the back end of a torpedo bomber. They fired out over the ocean until the ammunition ran out.

Over the next several months, Fireman First Class Luther Tidwell worked as security on transport ships that carried Marines from Honolulu to San Francisco. He made four round-trips between December, 1945 and February, 1946.

On June 5, 1946, Luther was discharged from the United States Navy. He arrived in Huntsville, Alabama on the train, and as he was driven back to his home in the community known as Big Cove, he waved at a pretty petite girl working out in the field. Beryl Broad had been a few years behind him in school and had a crush on him since the first time she met him when she was in the 7th grade. Before that day, he had hardly noticed the girl with beautiful blue eyes that would some day become his wife.

After two years in the Navy, Luther Tidwell went back to Madison County High School to finish his senior year. He was proud of his time in service, and came home with a new appreciation for family, home, and other people. But he never did learn how to swim.

About The Author

Jacquelyn Procter Gray is a native of Las Vegas, New Mexico and a graduate of New Mexico Highlands University. She writes for, and is Associate Editor of, *Old Tennessee Valley Magazine*. She has written for the *Historic Huntsville Quarterly*, the *Cumberland Presbyterian Vision*, and other publications. She is currently co-authoring a series of books about historic capital murders. Jacque lives in Huntsville, Alabama.

Printed in the United States
1153600001B/80

9 781403 384683